About the Author

Jessica Grundeman is a writer living on the South Coast of New South Wales, Australia, where she lives with her best friend and their chickens. She has wanted to be an author from a young age; at six-years-old, writing her first book, *Snowy the Dog*, on folded notebook paper. Unfortunately, the original copy of this masterpiece is currently unable to be located, so she hopes you enjoy this offering instead. Jessica grew up in southwest Sydney and graduated from Western Sydney University with a master's degree in education, majoring in English in 2014. She has been writing stories, poetry, and essays for most of her life; *All the People Who Died Here* is her first published novel. You can follow Jessica Grundeman on Facebook and Instagram.

All the People Who Died Here

Jessica Grundeman

All the People Who Died Here

Olympia Publishers
London

www.olympiapublishers.com
OLYMPIA PAPERBACK EDITION

Copyright © Jessica Grundeman 2024

The right of Jessica Grundeman to be identified as author of
this work has been asserted in accordance with sections 77 and 78 of
the Copyright, Designs and Patents Act 1988.

All Rights Reserved

No reproduction, copy or transmission of this publication
may be made without written permission.
No paragraph of this publication may be reproduced,
copied or transmitted save with the written permission of the publisher,
or in accordance with the provisions
of the Copyright Act 1956 (as amended).

Any person who commits any unauthorised act in relation to
this publication may be liable to criminal
prosecution and civil claims for damage.

A CIP catalogue record for this title is
available from the British Library.

ISBN: 978-1-80439-985-9

This is a work of fiction.
Names, characters, places and incidents originate from the writer's
imagination. Any resemblance to actual persons, living or dead, is
purely coincidental.

First Published in 2024

Olympia Publishers
Tallis House
2 Tallis Street
London
EC4Y 0AB

Printed in Great Britain

Dedication

For Craig,
because without you I wouldn't have been here to achieve my dream of writing a book. Thank you for saving my life and for helping me to live this new one.

Acknowledgements

Since I could read, I wanted to write, and once I could write, I wanted to be an author. For a long time, I thought that dream would never come true and now, after all these years, it has. I hope you enjoy my first published book.

Many people have helped me along this journey, and they deserve a thank you in writing, so that they may remember my gratitude for their input and support, as I remember the impact they had on me and my writing journey.

To my mother, Christine, who gave me my gift of words, teaching me to read and write at an early age and instilling in me my lifelong love of learning; that gift of literacy has shaped my entire world and I would not want it any other way. Of course, you have believed in me the entire time, even when I could not. I can never thank you enough for your unwavering belief and pride in my work.

To Kathy, my amazing beta reader extraordinaire, favourite aunt (Aunty Kaffy) and very dear friend: your reviews, encouragement, and suggestions made this book possible. I was blessed to have you on this journey with me.

To my father, Michael, my first storyteller, who made me want to be a storyteller too, I will be forever grateful for the "one more story" that you gave into to.

My year three and six teacher, Mr Bruce Farquhar, an amazing educator who few students will ever forget. You were always a great champion for my creative writing and your words of encouragement have never left me. I hope my book finds you somewhere.

My year eleven and twelve English teacher, Mrs Mary Chapman, a woman I will never forget. Your enthusiasm for literature certainly rubbed off on me, leaving me with an almost irrational love of Shakespeare. During my short teaching career, it was you I aspired to be. You taught me about myself and who I wanted to be just by being yourself in front of that classroom every day. Your encouragement of my writing has stayed with me all these years. The bar I still hold my work up to; *is it good enough for Mrs Chapman?* And I thank you for that.

To the team at Olympia Publishers, thank you for taking a chance on me and for all your hard work in producing my work to such a high standard.

Lastly, though most importantly, to Craig, how do I thank you for not just saving my life, but also for helping me to live it every day since then in the aftermath? Without you, this book would never have been written and my dream of being an author would never have been fulfilled. So, thank you for that, and for everything else.

Prologue

Stories are everywhere, every person, every place; every thing has a story to tell. A happy story soaring on the wings of its joy, a sad story drowning in its melancholy, a secret, a passion, a long-lost love, an unrequited love, a life waiting to be told.

Not everybody can hear them, but Lily can. She had been hearing their stories for as long as she could remember, sometimes a soft whisper, other times a roaring crescendo. The laments and the laudations, the closely guarded secrets, and whispered confessions finally set free, heard by no one but her. She had heard them all, all of the stories that set their tellers free. All of these stories became her familiars and all of their stories became her story. Now it was time for Lily's story to be told and in the telling would come Lily's own freedom.

The following story is compiled from Lily Lagniappe's archives and the recollections of Hannah Huntley, who helped Lily to compile a collection of her favourite and most memorable stories in her final days of being a story keeper and teller.

Chapter One: Lily's Gift

I

Lily Lagniappe was six years old the first time a spirit spoke to her; she was on the floor of her bedroom playing with some pink modelling clay when she first heard its voice. Like a whisper in her mind, it called her name to get her attention, and when it did, it told her a story. As the voice spoke, Lily could see what it was describing; stronger than imagination, it was a picture in her mind. Lily could see a child, a girl not much older than herself, her name was Kelly and she had red-brown hair in plaited pigtails, she wasn't wearing any clothes because it was bath time, the girl told her. Her brother, Tom, was there too; he was a bit younger, but Lily was given the sense that although Kelly was older than Tom in age and body, Kelly was younger in mind; something had happened to her before she was born that made her mind slow, her thoughts came to her through a fog, heavy like wet sand or mud, and her body didn't always do what her brain told it to do, or if it did it was delayed. Lily could see Kelly's Dad putting Tom and her in the bath together; he added a mermaid toy, a boat and a duck and then sat on the floor beside them. His thoughts were slow too, not heavy like Kelly's but messy and slurred; Kelly showed Lily a coffee table full of empty cans and bottles in explanation. The phone rang from the other room and at first their dad ignored it, it stopped ringing and then began again, he swore and stood up. "Tom, look after your sister, I'll be back to wash you both in a minute." He left the room.

Lily recognised the bathroom as her own and she knew that little kids shouldn't be in the bath without their mum or dad, so she ran in to tell them to get out, planning to get her own mum to help. Arriving in the bathroom, she was confused when it was empty. She heard Tom yelling, "Dad, Dad!" And getting no answer. Then Lily realised that the story she could see in her head had already happened, and all at once she knew that Kelly was dead, she had drowned and no one ever knew what had happened, because Tom couldn't speak properly yet. Lily knew, without even knowing the word yet, that Kelly had had a seizure; her dad was drunk and when he'd gone to answer the phone, he had gotten distracted and by the time he'd remembered that his kids were in the bath, it was too late. Tom had sat in the bath with his dead sister for an hour before his cries finally got through to his inebriated father. Tom hadn't learnt to speak yet when he got in that bath, and after that bath, he never did.

Lily left the bathroom and ran back to her bedroom. There were other voices in her head now, and she was being told a plethora of stories all at once whilst being shown thousands of images. It was overwhelming for the little girl, especially as most of the stories were about how people had died, and Lily understood that they were all people who had lived and died in her house. She put her modelling clay away and reached for a notebook and pencil. There she sat still and quiet, listening to the different voices.

"One at a time, please," she asked politely; nothing happened, so she asked again silently in her mind. The jumble slowed and Lily heard each story in turn; she worked as quickly as her little hands could to write them all down.

When she had finished and the voices were quiet, she went

to find her mother, who had been busy doing housework.

"Mummy, do you know a little girl drowned here in the bath? Her name was Kelly. Do you know an old man called Roger had lung cancer and coughed blood all over the shower and then died in there? Did you know that Nora died in her sleep? She was very old and she missed her fiancé who died in the Korean War, her heart just stopped one night. They are all the people who died here." Lily showed her shocked mother the pages she'd written.

"Lily, it's okay. No, I didn't know all of that, but I think we need to go see Grandma Carol," she said with calm resignation, knowing that it had always been a possibility that this day would come, though seeing as that it had skipped herself, hoping that it wouldn't. Although she felt the expected pang of maternal concern, she knew that Lily would be okay and that she would be able to handle the gift bestowed upon her. Lily had shown herself time and again, even at her tender age, to be intelligent and capable, almost fierce with independence, so pushing her motherly anxieties aside, she knew that she was right to be confident in Lily's ability to grapple victoriously with their family 'gift'.

Lily was excited to see her grandmother and proudly picked an outfit for herself. She didn't appreciate her mother trying to get her to pick something else, so in the end, her mother gave in and Lily wore yellow tights and a green pinafore with an orange cardigan over the top. Lily shook her head firmly at the proffered black Mary Janes and instead opted for the red patent leather ones.

Lily's grandmother was waiting outside for them when they arrived in the garden area of Broad Hill, the care home she lived in.

"Why are you out here, Grandma Carol?" Lily asked her; her enthusiasm for her outfit momentarily dwarfed her eagerness to tell her grandmother about the voices she could hear; she spun around to make sure her grandmother could see how good she looked in the clothes she had chosen for herself.

"It's quieter out here, Lily pad. Wow, I love what you're wearing today," Grandma Carol said, smiling at her granddaughter and giving her own daughter a knowing glance.

"I can still hear them; they're very loud and there's lots of them!" Lily exclaimed, her excitement holding a note of pride for her newfound talent.

"Really, all the way out here?" Grandma Carol confirmed, sounding slightly surprised.

"Yes, I think they're excited; they said you don't listen to them any more. So, they're frantic for me to hear their stories," Lily told her, her own excitement evident as she bounced up and down on the spot.

"I'm going to need a pen and paper," she added.

"Wow, you seem to be understanding what's going on, and it seems your gift is very strong." Grandma Carol sent Lily's mother to go get Lily a pen and some paper while they spoke.

"You have inherited a gift that runs in our family; it skips some people. Your mother doesn't have it, but I do and my mother does, though her mother doesn't. Like our black hair and blue eyes, you see?" Grandma Carol asked.

"Yes, I get it, but what do they want? Why are they telling us this stuff?" Lily answered, asking her own question.

"They're telling us because we're the only people who can hear them. They want their stories told. Some of them felt like they weren't heard when they were alive. They might have been ignored because they were different, or maybe they kept to themselves because they were sad; some people just aren't very good at life, so they die sad or with unfinished business. But even if they die happy, with nothing incomplete left behind, the allure of someone who can hear you is hard to ignore. Stories are a very strong thing, Lily, and so are their tellers and their keepers. These spirits are telling you their stories; this makes you the story keeper and when you write them down and tell them to other people, you are the storyteller, so that makes you very important," Grandma Carol explained.

"Well, I do love stories," Lily said, smiling.

Lily's mother had returned with the pens and paper, she handed them to Lily with a clipboard for her to lean on. Lily began writing while the two of them spoke.

"I'm so sorry, Helen. I really thought she wouldn't be able to hear them out here, but her gift is very strong," Grandma Carol said to her daughter.

"Don't apologise, Mum, it's not your fault. I'm just worried about her; six is too young to start being exposed to all this," she reasoned.

"Yes, it is, but she's a smart girl, and I'm here to guide her; I'll be able to teach her all the things she needs to protect herself from angry ones and how to turn them down and even off if gets too much," Grandma Carol said.

"You're right; she's going to need to learn a lot from you. It might be a good idea for you to come and stay with us or a while. Would that be, okay?" Helen asked her mother.

Carol was quiet for a moment; she looked over at Lily furiously writing away and said,

"Yes, she needs me to guide her for a bit. I'll just go inside and pack a few things and let my friends know I'll be away for a while; there are few of them that I better say a final goodbye to."

She winked, only half joking.

Grandma Carol returned home with Helen and Lily to give Lily the wisdom she was going to need to navigate her new life as the story keeper and teller.

At home, Lily put the pages she'd written at Broad Hill inside the notebook where she'd written Kelly, Roger and Nora's stories, adding the stories of Lydia, who'd lived her whole life in loneliness and died from loneliness, too. Martin and James who had both been soldiers in wars and who'd died from heart attacks many years later, with their horrible war memories never leaving them in peace. Paul, who'd worked in a bank and died with pneumonia. And Ava, Morty, Jonathan, Lucas, and Elizabeth, who'd all had marvellous lives, travelling and spending time with their large and extended families and who had all died from living at a very old age. Lily put the notebook away in her desk drawer; the desk had been her birthday present that year. Lily could be odd that way; where other six-year-old girls were asking for dolls or the latest thing that 'everyone had', she was asking for a desk to write at with notebooks to write in and a chair to sit in while doing it. She still had a penchant for a few of her dolls and a stuffed animal here and there, but the urge to make and record stories stirred in her stronger, perhaps a portent of what was about to occur: the gifts soon to be bestowed upon her and the storyteller she was to become.

The next morning, Lily sat for a moment on the edge of her bed, readying herself for the important lessons that her grandmother had come to teach her and the wisdom she was about to be gifted.

"Grandma Carol, do I need to write all the things down that you're going to teach me?" Lily asked her after a breakfast of toast and jam.

"No, Lily pad, that's already been done for us," her grandmother replied, producing a large and well-worn tome from the even larger carpet bag she'd brought with her the night before.

"Now, before we get started, there's some very important advice I need to give you; not everyone wants to know about all the people who lived and died in their house or wherever you might be with someone when you get told a story. Only tell them if they ask, but if you think it's very important for them to know, then you should ask them first and tell them that it's something they need to know about, then you can tell them," Grandma Carol told Lily, giving her the first tool to defend against the fear and rejection that a storyteller often encounters.

"Okay, Grandma, I'll do that, I promise. Now tell me about the book," Lily said eagerly.

"Good, now the book – this book has been passed down through our family, from the first one of us to have possessed the story keeper and teller gift hundreds of years ago. Each one of us adds to it if we discover something new, and we make sure the book is kept in good repair; if it starts to get too tattered or too hard to read, we have to transfer its pages to a new book, rewriting or typing them word for word without changing or missing anything, so that none of the wisdom is ever lost." Grandma Carol paused to sip her tea.

Lily looked at her much-loved grandmother and, for the first time, saw her as the wise woman she was, wisened by a lifetime of the gift of being able to hear and speak to the dead and by the generations of wisdom passed on to her. The lines on her face weren't just the years of her own life but countless other life stories told through her; the grey in her hair, too, was not just her own ageing but the ageing of the players from all the stories recounted to her.

"Is it hard, Grandma, to hear all their stories? Does it make you sad?" Lily had suddenly realised that this gift might not be just a gift; maybe, in time, it became a burden.

"It can be, but there are things in the book to help you with that. Writing the stories down helps because then they're not trapped inside of you. There are tricks we can do to tune them out if it's getting too much. You can even turn them down if it's too loud and you can make them louder if you need to hear them better." Grandma Carol smiled and began to flip through the book to show Lily examples of the things she was telling her.

"So, I can close my eyes and tell them in my mind that – I cannot hear you today, I am not able, you must go away. And that works?" Lily questioned, a little disbelieving.

"In most cases, yes, but in case it doesn't, that's why we carry these; the two combined make it work every time," her grandmother assured her as she emptied the contents of a large pouch in front of her, an array of crystals and jewellery spilling out.

Her grandmother explained each gemstone in turn, telling Lily how it could either protect her from evil spirits, negative energy, or bad intentions or how it could strengthen her gift and facilitate clearer communication between herself and the spirit world. She also explained that silver too can aid in reflecting away bad intentions and negative energy and that the evil eye symbol could be used for that as well.

Lily listened patiently to her grandmother's explanations, waiting until she had finished to ask a question about something she'd said.

"What's a psychic attack, Grandma?" Lily asked, scrunching her face up in confusion. For a moment, her grandmother was reminded that Lily, although well-spoken, bright for her age and in possession of a very strong psychic gift, was still only six years old. Her grandmother knew, though, that Lily's mediumship would make her mature faster than usual, and although that could be seen as sad, Lily was likely to have matured faster than usual anyway with her above-average intellect; being a medium was not Lily's only gift, the child had been reading and writing since the age of three and questioning the world around her from the moment she could speak.

"Well, there are lots of different types of abilities like ours, held by all different types of people; sometimes, bad people might use their gifts to try and hurt someone else, so we carry sapphire to protect ourselves," she explained.

"Now, these stones you must always carry with you, and to make their power stronger, there are seven pieces of jewellery you should also wear," Grandma Carol said, pointing to the pile of jewellery she'd emptied from the pouch. "An onyx and a sapphire ring, a cornelian and an aquamarine bracelet, a necklace with a silver chain holding a clear quartz point, another silver necklace holding the evil eye amulet and a silver ring. If you grow out of these ones, you can either carry them on your person in a pouch or you can replace them and keep these ones at home with the book. But always ensure you carry these with you. Because even if you never encounter an evil spirit or a bad-intentioned psychic, you will still be protected from the negativity and bad intentions of the living," she reasoned.

Lily picked up each piece of jewellery and put it on, and when her grandmother had gathered the crystals and put them back in their pouch, she took it from her and put it in the pocket of her jacket, actions that would become a daily ritual for the rest of her life, and for a little while even after that.

Over the years to come, Lily's grandmother guided her in her new gift. It had arrived strong and she was there to support her and answer her questions as it grew stronger; she gave her all the wisdom and guidance she had until her time was at an end, and when it was, she did not need to find a story keeper to tell her story to because her story had already been told to Lily.

II

For many long years, Lily lived with her gift; at times, it made life hard for her. The gift separated her, making her different from everyone else, and she soon found that even if she didn't tell people, keeping it a secret, people could still sense that she was different from them. Because of this, Lily was often left out; she was always picked last for teams and regularly left off birthday party invitation lists. But more than being left out or spending recess and lunches mostly alone, she was talked and gossiped about and so after a while, it wasn't just the other kids not including Lily or being mean to her; it became Lily segregating herself from them. She preferred to spend her time in the library or in a part of the playground where no one else played. Lily largely hid her gift, which led to her hiding her true self. Years of this resulted in it becoming hard for her to open up to people; she had few friends and relationships came and went. As did jobs, she never found herself able to choose a career path, and the menial jobs she supported herself with for a time, she was never able to commit to. The years of childhood spent speaking to spirits and hearing their stories grew through her teenage years, leaving an adult whose life had become the spirits' stories, leaving her own life somewhat lost in it all.

So eventually, instead of caring about what people thought, she embraced her gift harder and stopped hiding herself; in that way, she found the right people, a loving partner who never made her feel like she was weird and instead nurtured her and encouraged her gift, and a handful of friends who did the same. Life got a bit brighter, and she embraced being a story keeper and teller.

Living with her gift unhidden, practising it, even turning it into her profession, Lily helped people find out the histories of their homes or new buildings they had purchased, guiding them to find closure on mysterious deaths or family secrets until she had so many stories to keep and tell that the burden had grown too heavy, she was ageing and the gift had tired her out, she needed to retire and put the gift and the stories aside so that she could rest.

Lily had created a website where she advertised her services and people could contact her to request them; sometimes, people just wanted to ask her questions related to psychic powers and the spirit realm and she was happy to answer the questions that she could or direct them to websites or texts that might better help answer their queries. She used the website to publish a blog where she told some of the stories told to her by spirits. Though even with some of the stories passed on this way, there were many more still that needed to be told and an especial few that Lily knew needed to be presented in another way: a tangible form, physical, concrete and enduring. Before she could retire, Lily needed to ensure that this was done and as she hadn't produced any offspring for the gift to pass on to, she was hoping she could find someone else who possessed a gift of sixth sense who could maybe carry on her work, or at least benefit from the wisdom housed in the heirloom book holding the valuable insight of the wisened story keepers and tellers from her family line.

It was on this website, three days after deciding she needed to retire, that she received the following serendipitous email;

Dear Ms Lagniappe,

My name is Hannah Huntley. I suspect I may have some psychic abilities, and I am a student of parapsychology at Bellton University. I'm currently completing a research project on psychic experiences so that I can develop a dissertation for a PhD on the subject. I have followed your career since you launched your website in 1999 and I would be honoured if you'd agree to speak to me about the possibility of me interviewing you for my project.

Yours sincerely,
Hannah Huntley.

*

Dear Hannah,

Thank you for your email. I am certainly interested in speaking with you, though I'm sure I can offer you more than an interview; in fact, if you have some time to spare, I think we can be very helpful to each other.

Kind Regards,
Lily Lagniappe.

*

After a few back-and-forth emails confirming times and directions, Lily was set to meet Hannah in person so they could discuss some details and embark on Lily's pre-retirement project.

Lily was already seated in the Number 9 Café when Hannah arrived. She watched her walk past the pop art and Andy Warhol reproductions, the black and silver stools at the milk bar counter, to the patent red leather booth in the back where Lily was waiting. Hannah's hair was smoothed carefully into a sleek low ponytail, a crisp white tailored shirt over black slim-leg pants and low heels, stylish but sensible like she was going to a job interview. Lily would come to learn over their time together that today's outfit was only a slight variation on her usual style – sometimes wearing more casual shoes or shirt, or even a more relaxed hairstyle, but always keeping to her tailored manner of dressing, as though she was trying to lend a level of professionalism to the field she was desperately trying to establish as credible.

"Hello, Hannah, nice to finally meet you," Lily said warmly as Hannah arrived in front of her.

"Yes, you too. This place is amazing; I can't believe I've never heard about it before!" Hannah exclaimed as she looked around appreciatively at the retro kitsch décor, hiding her nervousness well.

"Yeah, it really is; it's somewhat of a hidden treasure. I used to live around the corner from here, so I guess I got let in on the secret." Lily smiled as Hannah sat down.

"So, you said in your email that if I have some time, we can help each other; what do you have in mind?" Hannah asked, getting straight into it and trying not to look too awe-struck as she sat in front of the woman who had become an idol to her.

"Well, you said you've been following my website since '99, so I guess you know I've been doing what I do for a long time, and you've probably noticed that I haven't updated my blog in a while and that I've not been active on the website. I suppose you could say I'm winding things up. I just feel like it's time to step away from what I do or step down, I guess you could say," Lily offered as an opening.

"You mean you're retiring?" Hannah asked, the shock in her voice hinting at her disappointment.

"Yes, I guess that's the best way to describe it," Lily agreed, nodding without further elaborating.

"But you're not even that old," Hannah protested politely.

"I've never revealed my age in my blog or on my website. I'm older than I look, you know," Lily said with a smile.

"Then why are you retiring?" Hannah prodded.

"Being old isn't the only reason people retire. Having a Sixth sense is very draining. But aside from that, my husband isn't well, and I want to take care of him. The stories are important, but he is more important; his story is the most important one to me, so it's time I retire and focus on that," Lily told her as plainly as she could.

Hannah sensed that there was something Lily wasn't telling her, but at the same time, she felt that eventually, her secret would be known to her, so she answered, "Okay, that's understandable." And smiled the smile of sympathy that went with being told that someone's husband was ailing.

"Now you mentioned that you think you may have some of your own psychic abilities. Let's talk about that before I give you my proposal," Lily said as she shook her arm to shift her bracelets into a more comfortable position.

"Well, I've always believed in all things supernatural and sometimes I dream things or sense them before they happen. And sometimes I dream about dead people, family or friends, but it's more than a dream, it's like they're visiting me, like they're really there and they tell me things, stories and secrets... that sort of thing," Hannah tried to explain with a bit of gesticulation.

"Is that why you're studying parapsychology?" Lily asked her, hoping to elicit more of who Hannah was.

"Partially." She nodded, agreeing, and then continued with a more detailed explanation. "I thought if I could understand the field more, it might help me understand what I have and maybe grow it, but I'm also fascinated with the whole subject. There are so many misconceptions and such a wealth of misinformation around anything to do with the paranormal and psychic abilities. I'd love to be part of a more concrete study, with credible research and solid findings published in a professional manner." Hannah's face lit up with the intensity of her passion. And she smiled, a little abashed that she'd let her ardour carry her away.

"Well, that's great! I'm sure work like that could help with the hurdles faced by people who possess these types of gifts: the discrimination, the fear, being made 'other'," Lily replied, thinking to herself that she'd found the right person.

"I think I have to confess that there's a bit more to it; another reason that I wanted to study parapsychology is you. I guess you could call me a fan." Hannah smiled awkwardly and averted her gaze down to the table.

Continuing, she said, "Once I found your blog and website, I saw this professional woman, who was maybe a bit quirky like me, who had been teased and left out because of her beliefs and gifts; I could relate to that, although I'm not as gifted as you, I guess I hoped that one day I might be. I've looked up to you; maybe I even wanted to be you." Now Hannah's face coloured, heat rushed to her cheeks as she fished in her handbag for a photograph and, having found it, held it across the table so that Lily could see. The picture showed Hannah, somewhere between late teens and early YA, her own honey-brown hair hidden under a long black wig and blue contact lenses, giving her eyes the same hue as Lily's. She was dressed in a white boho-style dress with a woven tan belt hitched low on her hips, her jewellery akin to that which Lily wore; the outfit making her a simulacrum of Lily in early photos of her on her website in the style of dress she had favoured in the late 90s and early '00s – when the bright colours of childhood had given way to the more subdued selections of an adult.

"A real photo? A real-life printed-out photograph instead of a digital one?" Lily remarked, leaving the subject matter aside for the moment.

"Yes, I like real, physical photos that I can hold onto. I spend so much time with my head in the incorporeal studying the intangible that I like a solid reality that I can touch, something to hold on to," Hannah explained, her voice hinting at a truth Lily recognised well: the weight of a life lived with the ethereal.

"Halloween party?" Lily asked, circling back around to what was in the photo and trying not to sound like she was teasing her.

"Not quite; it was a fancy dress party; you had to go as your hero. I can't believe I showed you this." Hannah laughed, shaking her head at herself.

Now it was Lily's turn to be embarrassed. "Wow, I'm a bit speechless. I didn't know I had fans – are you my groupie?" Lily couldn't help but to tease her a little bit.

"Umm…" Hannah fumbled to find words to explain herself.

"I'm joking, sorry, I'm actually really flattered and I'm happy if I helped you feel better when you were made fun of for believing in supernatural things," Lily told her.

"Thank you because you really did; you made me believe that it's okay to believe in the paranormal and to believe in myself. Even though we'd never met before today, I always felt like you were my friend," Hannah admitted, toying with her ponytail that had made its way over her shoulder.

"Well, I guess I am a friend to all who are open to exploring sixth senses and the world beyond our own, and I would say that now we have met, we are friends," Lily told her, leaning across the table to touch her hand.

Lily, believing that she had found the right person to help her finish her work before retiring completely, told Hannah, "Now, what I'm proposing is this: I have three more jobs booked; they'll be my last ones. I'm asking you to come along with me and take record of what happens, take photos, record me telling you what stories I get, or write them down. I find I've been forgetting some details lately, so you'll be helping me out with that by taking it all down. But before that, I have a few jobs I'd like to revisit; I'd need you to come along with me and let me tell you the stories while we take some photos. These stories, along with my last three jobs, are going to be part of a book I'm publishing. This book is very important, and it needs to be done so that the spirits in the stories told are able to rest. Every story that I've ever been told by spirits has either been recorded or written down. I have an enormous archive; some of these already stood out to me more than others, but when I decided to retire, I went into my archive – the room I keep all of the stories in, and these particular stories were still whispering to me and some of them were screaming. Their spirits aren't at rest yet and I believe that publishing these stories in an actual book will help them be able to finally do so. These particular spirits have hung around because of their stories; they can't pass on or rest fully until their stories are heard by more than just me, for whatever reason – the reason doesn't matter, it just is – they need people to know their stories. And that's what it's always been about for me; that's why I do the work I do. I could silence the voices enough to ignore them, but I couldn't live with myself; their stories need to be told so that they can rest.

"You can use whatever you like from this time to support your research or make part of your dissertation for your PhD. I can also answer whatever questions I can that you have about my work and gifts or the gifts you may have," Lily gave her long explanation.

"Okay, yes, that sounds amazing, and I do have a lot of questions for you about your gifts. Do you mind if we start with those now?" Hannah produced a large notepad from her bag and placed her phone ready to record next to it, mentally pinching herself to make sure she wasn't dreaming.

"Not at all; I'm eager to get started because I only have a limited amount of time to get the book done," Lily told her.

"You're on a deadline?" Hannah asked.

"Something like that," Lily agreed, with that smile again.

"I guess we should order something if we're going to be here for a while," Hannah suggested and so a coffee and a hot chocolate were ordered along with some fries and toasted sandwiches, which served as an aside to their conversation, though Lily mostly just played with hers.

Hannah asked Lily how her gift worked if she could just walk into a place and know who lived and died there. Lily told her that she can do this in most places, but not all; not every spirit or house or place has a story to tell, and not every place always wants to give up their story, but she can usually get some sense, some kind of idea if she concentrates hard enough.

"And what if you don't want to hear one of the stories, like if it's too dark or maybe you're sad yourself that day – like maybe you've got your own stuff going on and it's too much to deal with the stories; what do you do? Can you block it out completely?"

Hannah asked, the idea of an onslaught of noise that couldn't be controlled disturbing her.

"My grandmother taught me things to use to make the voices quieter, and yes, I can even block them out completely; it takes a lot of energy and concentration, but if I need to, it can be done; it's not an attack of uncontrollable noise. But sometimes it's very soft and it's easier to silence," Lily explained.

"It must be hard sometimes, being the only one who can hear them," Hannah said.

"Yes, it is sometimes, but it *is* a gift and most of the time, it feels that way – but you're right, at times, it does feel like it's all too much and that's when I use what my grandmother taught me." Lily smiled as she remembered the wise woman. She then took a few moments to explain to Hannah about the concentrating, the crystals and the incantations.

"Like spells? "Hannah exclaimed when Lily had finished.

"Kind of, I guess. They usually rhyme, so I've always thought of them as little poems or songs." She smiled, nodding.

"What about types of..." Hannah struggled for the word, "ghosts, spirits, entities?" she shrugged, not knowing the correct term.

"I usually use 'spirits', but you're right, there are different kinds," Lily agreed and then proceeded to explain to Hannah that;

"Spirits are like what most people would call a ghost; they are energy left behind, often they have unfinished business, so they use their energy to appear to people or communicate in other ways. Some spirits have a lot of energy and can appear however they'd like to, making themselves younger or in better shape than when they died, and they can move around to different places. Others don't have much energy, so can only appear as they looked at the moment they died. And with less energy they are more like what people traditionally think of as ghosts that haunt a particular place, thing or person. These entities are mostly benevolent, wishing only to tie up loose ends or deliver messages," Lily said, breaking down to Hannah her experience.

"What about evil spirits, demons and poltergeists?" Hannah questioned, her eyes wide and excited, the lilt in her voice exposing her hunger for knowledge on anything concerning her favourite subject.

"They are pretty much the opposite end; they are malevolent because their intent is evil. Mostly, they are angry and violent and they can cause physical damage to things and, in some cases, people. It's hard for me to quantify what the difference is between a demon and a poltergeist, but in my experience, a demon is usually older and often rooted in the corruption of some form of religion. Whereas a poltergeist is usually created by a great injustice or some terrible thing that has happened to the person in life, often tied with what led to their death," Lily said, trying to be as specific as the subject matter allowed.

"I can't say for certain if there are or aren't other types of entities created by the energy that remains when someone dies. Likely there are, but I'm not familiar with any others and there aren't any others mentioned in the book that has guided the story keepers and tellers in my family," Lily finished her long explanation.

"Story keepers and tellers, is that what you call yourselves?" Hannah asked.

"That's what it's been called in my family; that's what my grandmother called me when the gift came to me; it's a form of mediumship, really, but story keeper/teller is what it's always been called in my family," Lily clarified, sounding tired from all the talking.

"Well, it looks like they're getting ready to close, and I really should be getting home, so I guess we'd better call it a day for now," Lily explained to Hannah.

"Oh wow, I didn't realise it had gotten so late; it's dark outside!" Hannah said, amazed that so much time had passed; she had been so transfixed by Lily's words that she hadn't even realised she had been.

"I have a few things to organise and then we can start our project. I'll email you the details over the next few days and we'll get started." Lily smiled and the two exchanged goodbyes. Lily went home, certain she had found the person she needed to help her complete her important project and be able to retire and Hannah returned to her university residence room, certain she had the key to a prize-winning PhD dissertation.

Chapter Two: Nobody Died Here, Norman's Story

I

Three days after Lily and Hannah met in the No.9 Café, they began Lily's project.

They arrived at 88 White Pine Drive in the early afternoon and although it was a bright, warm day, Lily felt neither of those things, heavy with the chill of the dark story about to be told.

Lily hesitated before initiating an exit from her black vintage Beetle, mentally readying herself to relive the macabre tale. Hannah took the time to start a voice recording on her phone and asked a few questions.

"How did you come about this job?" she asked, using Lily's hesitation to gather some establishing background information to be used later for her PhD.

"I was contacted by a young woman who'd inherited a house from her late aunt a few months earlier. She didn't have the heart to sell it, so she'd been trying to rent it out, but none of the tenants would stay. After trying to stay in the house herself, she understood why no one wanted to live there, and now, suspecting that the house was haunted, she enlisted my help to get some answers. See, the house itself scares everyone, the owner has never had any luck renting it out long-term, and every sale has fallen through. It's been left vacant for a long time; I think she's just let it sit empty now, except for the ghosts," Lily answered, the mention of ghosts foreshadowing what was to come, if only symbolically.

"And was it haunted?" Hannah asked, noticing some movement in the upstairs window from the corner of her eye.

"Not in the usual sense, but the answer to what was going on in the house, in reality, was really quite frightening. This story is probably one of the ones that scared me the most. Out of all of them, it stayed with me, and that's why I've picked it to go in the collection."

"They're still here?" Hannah asked the apprehension in her voice not quite hiding her enthusiasm.

"Norman is; he never left. Marion never truly was here after her death, but she's here through Norman's delusion. I can feel them both," Lily said with sadness for the restless souls.

"Well, let's get the photos done so I can hear this story and find out who Norman and Marion are!" Hannah said, patting her camera bag, her enthusiasm now erasing her apprehension.

"Is that a real camera, like an actual camera? A real camera like the real photos, right?" Lily asked.

"Yep, sure is; maybe I'm quirky or old school, I don't know, but I just like the feel of it. I think it's nice to have a camera that's only a camera fulfilling its purpose without having to be all fancy by being a phone and an alarm clock and all that other stuff," Hannah said, letting an embarrassed smile escape, as she did sometimes when she felt she'd gotten accidentally carried away.

"Well, I think that's a great quirk to have Hannah. Now let's make a start." Lily smiled at her.

They exited Lily's car and Hannah snapped a few photos of the front of the house and a blackened spot on the ground that Lily indicated to.

"Get some of that window on the top floor," Lily instructed.

Hannah turned to do so, for a moment, thinking she saw a figure there, but it was gone so quickly that she couldn't be certain if it had been there at all. When she turned back, she couldn't see Lily anywhere.

"Over here!" Lily waved from the now-open doorway. "Let's do this quickly; I don't want to stay here too long," she said, motioning for Hannah to come inside. What she didn't tell her was that she didn't want to stay too long because she didn't want Norman to notice they were there. Lily had never been certain what type of entity he might have turned into; she feared that it was likely a malevolent one. One that might be too powerful for the tokens of protection she carried.

Lily took Hannah upstairs to the window she'd instructed her to photograph from the outside and told her to get photos of the black mark on the floor beneath it. She then led her to a manhole cover that hid a set of folding stairs leading to a small attic.

"Please get some pictures of that," Lily said softly, her voice having adopted a calming, hushed tone once they'd entered the house.

"Do you want me to go up in there and get some pictures?" Hannah's apprehension was back, but her curiosity was almost stronger.

"No, that's okay. Just a couple of the manhole cover is fine. I was shown a very clear vision of what it looked like up there when I was here doing the job; I think I'll be able to describe it well enough to my readers," Lily told her. It was much too risky to go up there now; if Norman was angry, he was angry in there.

"Let's go. I don't want to tell you the story in here." They went back to Lily's car, where she proceeded to tell Hannah Norman's story.

Lily settled herself in her seat and took a breath before beginning.

"Norman Perkins had loved Mrs Leigh from the first moment he saw her, a rainy day in 1989 when he was ten years old, and his regular teacher Mrs Mars had been absent. The beautiful, porcelain-skinned Mrs Leigh had taken her place. The first thing he had noticed was her red hair, wavy but cropped close to her head, so elegant, so beautiful, he became enamoured instantly. Norman stared at her from beneath his dark hair, pushing it to the side of his angular face so that he could better see her, a devilish smile spreading beneath a nose that dwarfed the rest of his features.

Mrs Leigh was his teacher for three days whilst Mrs Mars was sick, and on the third day, it was class photos. Usually, a substitute teacher wouldn't be in the class photo, but Norman had other ideas; he had hatched a plan.

"Oh no!" cried Norman in great distress. "Mrs Mars always stands next to me for photos because I get so nervous; I'll be so scared without her!" He stomped his foot and began to cry. Some of the other children spoke amongst themselves, saying what a baby he was and how they didn't like him.

Mrs Leigh shushed them and went to Norman, telling him,

"It's okay, Norman; I'll stand next to you and make sure you're not nervous; there's nothing to be scared of." She smiled at him and used a tissue from her pocket to wipe his face.

The class took their photo without incident, Norman beaming and overflowing with love for his beloved Mrs Leigh.

On the fourth day, when Mrs Mars returned, Norman was inconsolable; he was sullen and surly for three days, lost in deep agony over the loss of his beloved until the class photos arrived. As soon as he saw the image of Mrs Leigh, he became all sweetness and light.

The photo printing company had listed the substitute teacher's full name, Marion Leigh, instead of the usual initial and surname. Norman was overjoyed to learn this piece of information about his beloved Mrs Leigh, and it carried him through the whole term until Mrs Mars was absent again. These were to become the happiest days of not just Norman's schooling but of his whole childhood and adolescence, the days when his regular teacher was absent and Mrs Leigh was called to fill in. He lived for those days, and in between them, the weekends and holidays, all his private idle hours, he gazed at her picture. Of course, he had cut out the rest of the class, keeping only the small rectangle that contained just he and his beloved. He gazed at it, daydreaming, dreaming up many elaborate fantasies containing her and even more elaborate ones containing the two of them. These fantasies grew through his childhood, intensifying with his burgeoning adolescence until they became the matured and fully developed dreams of a thoroughly infatuated man. Having learnt her full name when he was in year five had made it a lot easier for him to keep track of her. Norman knew where Mrs Leigh lived, he knew her phone number, he knew what kind of car she drove, he was able to track which schools she worked at, and he knew when her husband died. Norman kept all of his Mrs Leigh information to himself; he never spoke of her to anyone; his love, his obsession, was very well hidden but also very well-tended and over all the years that had passed since that first day he had seen her in 1989, his love for her had never once dwindled, it had instead thrived. More than thrived, it had flourished. And in fact, it had done more than flourish; it had proliferated, becoming an indestructible force in his life that overrode and devoured everything else.

So, thirty years later, when Mrs Leigh's body was dropped off by the coroner at the morgue he worked at, Norman knew it was her before he even looked at the paperwork, and he knew what he had to do. It was the reason he had trained for and taken the job at the morgue, all in anticipation of this day. He had waited for this day, longing for it. He had carried out the duties of preparing a body for burial or cremation many times before, but this time, he had rehearsed the steps, the slightly different steps, many times in his head.

Norman took extra care with Mrs Leigh, whom he wouldn't begin to refer to as Marion, for another five years. He washed her very gently and sombrely, forcing himself to become disassociated and detached whilst he drained her body of blood and replaced it with embalming fluid, this time savouring the stinging hit of the sharp chemical stench. And whilst he drained her chest and abdominal cavities of gasses, he allowed himself to picture instead the life they would soon have together. He propped up his prized photograph on the bench so he could better picture her more youthful, living face as he set her facial features. Lovingly, he set the eye caps in place with skin-coloured glue. Then he closed her mouth, the first time he had had his fingers so close to her lips. Securing her jaw hurt him deeply and he began to cry quietly as he pulled the suture string through her lower jaw and up through the gums of the top teeth; the popping sound it made when the suturing needle pierced her flesh threatened to break him so he pictured her wiping his face when he had cried before the class photo, and he was able to finish the job.

Lucky for Norman, no one else seemed to love Mrs Leigh as much as he did. Her husband had died years earlier and there was no family left who cared enough for a funeral; her body was scheduled for a direct cremation, and although Norman understood that sometimes followers of the Buddhist faith or those who don't follow any religion opted for a direct cremation, he knew that Mrs Leigh was none of those, though he doubted that the presence of any grieving family or plans for an elaborate funeral would have changed his plans anyway, just complicated them.

Norman had become so lost in his work and his daydreaming of a future with Mrs Leigh that he had forgotten that another diener was due to start work. He only had Mrs Leigh half inside the body bag he was using for transport when he heard Alan walk in. Alan was whistling some inane tune; the brash inappropriateness of it both for their place of work and the disrespect to Mrs Leigh produced an anger in Norman that he had not felt before.

Norman took in a deep breath and compelled himself to ask, "Hi Alan, did you ride your bike or drive to work today?"

"Oh, hey Norman, nah, I walked." He continued whistling.

Good. Before Norman had time to think, he had reacted, swiping up the baseball bat kept behind the morgue's back door for 'just in case'.

The deniers used to joke amongst themselves that it was for just in case one of the cadavers turned into a zombie, triggering a zombie apocalypse. But really, it was for 'just in case' one of the many freaks and weirdos who skulked around the premises in the early hours of the morning tried something sinister or disgusting.

It hadn't even registered to Norman that the bat was in his hand, but there it was, and there he was, reacting to Alan's stupid whistle. He hit the younger man once and with great force over the back of his head. A startled kind of 'Ooff' omitted from Alan as though the air had been knocked out of him, the force of the blow swinging him around before he crumpled to the floor, the smack of it snapping Norman from his trance-like state as he stared down at Alan's twitching body.

The anger wasn't subsiding; he felt no shock or remorse, and instead, he saw a fantastically convenient opportunity presented to him. He spent a quick minute wiping down and replacing the bat behind the back door and then kicked Alan aside to check the floor around and under him for blood; seeing none, he concluded that the blow he'd given him had caused only internal bleeding, which made everything much easier for Norman. And although he couldn't be sure if Alan was completely dead yet, he didn't have the time to worry about that; he needed to finish his task and get Mrs Leigh home as soon as possible.

He grabbed Alan's arms and pulled them up over his head, dragging him towards the cremation chamber. Usually, the bodies went in inside a coffin, feet first, but this wasn't usual circumstances, and Norman just needed the job done. He stuffed Alan as best could onto the insertion trolley and sent him into the chamber. There may have been a slight stirring and a few small sounds coming from Alan, but these were ignored by Norman as he shut the chamber doors and fired up the gas for cremation.

Norman went back to Mrs Leigh while the chamber heated up and the cremation commenced. He ignored any sounds that may or may not have been a screaming Alan, instead humming himself a happy tune that drowned out the screaming sounds as he secured her properly inside the body bag and moved her to the back seat of his car for transport, laying her as neatly and comfortably for her as he could.

"Just wait there, Mrs Leigh; I won't be much longer, then I'll take you home; we're going to have such a nice time together, I promise." He smiled and kissed her forehead through the bag.

Shutting the car door, he stepped back from the vehicle, making sure nothing looked strange. Satisfied it didn't, he returned to the cremation chamber to wait for the cremation to be complete.

While he did this, he double-checked the roster and found that, as he had thought, there was no one else due in for another six hours. He waited three, enough time for Alan's body to be reduced to ashes and some cooling to have commenced. The ashes were still hotter than usually would be, but again, these were not usual circumstances. Norman found the plain, ugly, cheapest urn that the uncaring family had chosen for his beloved Mrs Leigh and scraped Alan's ashes into it; he sealed it as was expected and attached a note to it saying, 'Mrs Marion Leigh' and left it in the 'to be collected cupboard'. He correctly filed all the paperwork that had accompanied Mrs Leigh, cleaned out the cremation chamber and then phoned Mr Harper, the morgue's manager and told him that Alan hadn't shown up for work and his phone was going straight to voice mail. Mr Harper told him to lock up and go home; the next shift would be there soon enough.

Norman smiled; he was finally taking his beloved Mrs Leigh home, no, to *their* home.

When he finally shut the door behind them, he leaned his back against it and released a relieved sigh. Taking in the room, his elated excitement at finally being inside her house was writ large upon his face with a grin he could not wipe off and a euphoria that brought new life to his eyes. He had only ever been able imagine how the inside of her home was decorated from the years he had spent admiring it, taking comfort in it and her from afar. Now he could hardly believe that he was regarding it from within and her from up close, his comfort now immediate. He was delighted to find that many of his imaginings had been right;

her home was beautiful, so tastefully decorated and he revelled at being inside of it with her after all those years of watching from a distance.

For three months, they lived peacefully together. Norman would dress Mrs Leigh according to the season and they would spend many happy hours together, talking over dinner or enjoying one of Mrs Leigh's favourite shows. Finally, the day came that Norman was both fearing and expecting, he already had a plan in place. It was probable that Mrs Leigh had left her house to someone and eventually that someone would come to claim it. Norman's plan made none of this matter, and so he and Marion were able to continue enjoying each other's company for many years. Norman was so happy inside the life he made himself with Mrs Leigh; it was bliss beyond his wildest imagination, and even the fact that she was dead did little to diminish it at all.

Norman's plan needed to make use of a hidden, confined space, an almost secret place, somewhere that people forgot about and ignored; a place where people living in the house went about their days without thinking about – so much so that even when things went bump in the night, they would either explain it away by concluding it was an innocent house sound emanating from somewhere or else jumping to the conclusion that a ghost was the culprit; all of which worked well for Norman. And seeing as that there were many hours from Norman's childhood that made such places a familiar comfort to him, it was much less of a problem for Norman to live in such a place as it may have been for others, and with the company of Marion, it was divine.

II
Somewhere Between 1983–1992

What had started as a punishment eventually turned into a sanctuary, a sanctuary that was to prepare him for the most significant and joyful years of his life.

"Norman, I told you what would happen if you were a dirty little bastard again!" his mother, Virginia, screamed at him, her face red, nostrils flaring, her whole body trembling with rage as she circled her bony fingers around Norman's tiny wrist and pulled him towards the linen cupboard. Norman screamed, but only in his mind.

"*No, Mummy, please, I didn't mean to!*" he begged silently. He had learnt from experience with his mother, beloved by him but now more feared, that it was better for him to stay silent and do all of his crying and protesting inside his head. She ripped open the cupboard door and pulled piles of towels and sheets from within, swinging Norman by his wrist into the small cavity between the bottom shelf and the one above it; he tucked himself up, knees to his chest, elbows to his side so that he fit better and didn't enrage her further. He stayed quiet, ignoring the wet pants that were now cold and sticking to him.

Before she shut and locked the door, she leaned towards him, putting her lips close to his ear and bleated, "You stay there until you're dry, you filthy disgusting thing!" Then she slammed the door to the cupboard and slid in place the lock she had fitted for the sole purpose of locking Norman in there.

Confined in the cupboard, Norman wasn't scared; he felt safer in there, away from her. But it was small and cramped, and his back would end up aching, an ache that would eventually turn into a screaming agony that engulfed his whole body. Sometimes, he would cry in there, but he would do it softly so that she didn't hear and leave him in there longer. Hours, sometimes whole days locked inside the linen cupboard awoke an internal struggle in Norman; yes, the hours locked up resulted in physical pain, but they also kept him safe from his mother's rage, which was apt to turn more violent, with blows being rained on him from her hand, or whatever she found useful close by, be it a kitchen utensil, a book, a belt, the broom, or some such other item. Eventually, Norman came to the conclusion that whether in or out of the cupboard, he would end up in pain, but at least inside the cupboard, he felt safe, and he didn't have to look at her face contorted with rage and hatred, screaming vile things about him. It was peaceful in there.

And soon after that realisation, he didn't mind the cupboard so much any more.

When he grew too big to fit in any of the cupboards in the house, the screaming and hitting became worse; around this time, Norman found his own solution; he would take himself to the storage space in the roof of his home and spend his time there. He eventually found ways to come and go from the roof cavity without his mother even noticing. He would sneak down to gather food, bathe and do other things he needed to; his mother never questioned where he had been because she had noticed; she knew where he'd been spending his time, and it pleased her. Virginia believed her son to be a dirty, disgusting thing and he deserved to live in a place meant for discarded things, insects and rats, so Norman had his safe sanctuary and his mother had what she wanted: her dirty boy out of her sight.

Many, Many Years Later – *(years after Mrs Leigh had been brought home, and years after Norman had had to enact his plan):*

"It's a little bit cold today, Mrs—"

"Marion! I've told you a thousand times, Norman, it's been a long, long time since I was your teacher; we sleep in the same bed; you can call me Marion now!" Norman heard Marion's body tell him.

"Sorry, I'm so sorry, I just keep forgetting; it's a bit cold today, *Marion*," he corrected himself and showed her the shawl he'd bought for her before tucking it gently around her slender shoulders.

"Why, thank you, Norman darling, it's beautiful." Norman watched Marion smile as she admired the black velvet fabric embroidered intricately with flowers and paisley motifs, running the tasselled fringe through her long fingers.

"You're very welcome, Marion; as soon as I saw it, I knew it was meant for you; the roses so beautifully match the hue of your beautiful hair." Norman turned and rummaged in a large paper bag, unpacking some premade sandwiches, a packet of salted potato chips, a packet of chocolate biscuits and a bottle of lemonade.

"I see you've brought my favourite for lunch for us. You look after me so well." Norman leant to place a gentle kiss on Marion's cheek before setting out their lunch. He had just picked up a sandwich when he heard voices; he held one finger to his lips, widening his eyes at Marion and froze in place for a moment, listening.

"Well, like I told you on the phone, it's been three years and we haven't been able to keep the same tenants for longer than two or three months; one family left after three weeks! I tried living here once and the same things happened to me!" the first voice said.

"And what are their reasons for leaving? What do they complain about?" a second voice answered, asking a question.

"It's like we already talked about; they hear things moving around at night, things are moved around in the house or missing. A lot of them say they feel like there's someone here. My first thought was that the house was haunted; this was my aunt's house and she died five years ago," the first voice paused for a second. "Is it haunted Mrs Lagniappe?" it continued.

"Please, call me Lily," the second voice answered.

What Norman couldn't see was Lily standing straight, her arms by her side, her head tilted slightly upwards as she panned her head slowly around the lounge room they stood in. "Let me walk around the house a bit and see what I can get; no one's speaking to me yet. Did your aunt die here?"

"No, I think she died in the hospital," Marion's niece answered, Norman couldn't see her hair that was red like Marion's and her eyes that were just like her aunt's.

"Hmm," Lily said, taking big steps around the room, tilting her head from side to side, touching walls, then she began walking like she was following something or being led; her head snapped straight up to the ceiling, a scene filling her head; in the close confines of the roof cavity, not quite an attic, but more than a crawl space, a home had been made, and a life was being lived in it. Lily could see a bed that had been fashioned from a mattress and some blankets; there was a low table covered with a delicate lace tablecloth, a half-eaten meal spread upon it, ham and cheese sandwiches set out on China plates with a rose pattern, potato chips in an antique crystal bowl, chocolate biscuits spread on a vintage yellow platter sporting moulded ceramic sunflowers, a bottle of lemonade with some poured into crystal wine glasses that matched the antique bowl. And pulled up to this spread was an old pink lounge that had in earlier years been a part of the house's furnishings. Lily saw an old woman wrapped in a patterned shawl, her hair a vibrant red that was maintained meticulously to be kept that way. It wasn't until she saw Norman next to her on the lounge that she knew what the house had been trying to tell her.

"Something's wrong, no one died here!" Lily exclaimed, the look of horror on her face matching the horror in her voice.

She ran back to Marion's niece, Mary and, taking her by the wrist, ran with her out of the front door, imploring her to lock it behind them. Lily didn't let Mary's wrist free until they were outside the locked front gate.

Norman couldn't hear them speaking any more, but he had heard enough, and he was watching; he could see them outside the gate.

Mary was looking at Lily in confusion. "What, what did you see?" she asked her.

"I'm not sure how to tell you this." Lily took a big breath and continued.

"Mary, your Aunt Marion is still here, not in spirit; she didn't speak to me; it was the house that spoke to me. Your Aunt's spirit passed over when her body died; she had no unfinished business or wrongs to right. Her spirit is at rest, but her body is still in that house, and so is someone else; I can't quite get who it is. The house doesn't know the person, but I think we need to call the police. Tell them there's an intruder hiding in the roof of your aunt's home and that he's dangerous," Lily told her.

"What do you mean her body's still in the house? I have her

ashes!" Mary exclaimed, incredulous.

Lily made the call to the police and then continued to explain to Mary. Norman watched through the vent in the roof cavity and pieced together what was going on.

"It's hard to say because I can't reach your aunt's spirit, but I was able to sense some information from the house; see, I'm not exactly a psychic. Usually, the spirits tell me things, but I can see or know some things that have happened in a place. The house showed me an old photograph; it looked like a young student and a teacher," Lily said.

"My Aunt was a relief teacher; she filled in for teachers who were sick," Mary told her, excited.

"Like I said, the house doesn't know the person, but it can tell me things about them. I think it was saying that the person in there now was a student of your aunt's. I'm definitely getting that he loved, no, not past tense, *loves,* he loves your aunt; in his mind, she never died; he has her body in the house. I could see through the ceiling; they're in the roof cavity. He's been living in there with her, coming and going; that's the disturbances your tenants have been experiencing; he's been stealing food and little objects from them." Lily's face looked like she was far away as she again brought up the images she'd been shown in the house, Norman and Marion eating together, listening to the radio together, sleeping side by side in a bed Norman had fashioned for them out of a mattress and some blankets. And conversations, two-sided conversations.

"He carries out conversations with her; he truly believes she speaks back to him, in his mind it is real, in his mind he is living with his wife, who loves him.

"I'm sorry, Mary; I know this must be hard to hear," Lily

said as she noticed Mary wiping away some tears.

"I'm sure it probably doesn't help, but he has treated her very well; he hasn't violated her body, don't worry about that, he had thought about it, I'll be honest with you, but he was very careful about keeping her body preserved. I'm not sure that he would be able to perform in that manner anyway," Lily said tactfully.

"You mean sexually?" Mary asked. "You mean he didn't fuck her dead body?" she said angrily.

"Yes, that's what I'm saying; sorry, I thought you might think he had, but he hasn't. I wanted to ease your mind of that idea," Lily explained.

"But you think he's dangerous? You rushed me out of there and called the police," Mary reasoned.

"I'm not a hundred per cent sure, but I did get some flashes of something; I think he's killed in the past, he's obviously mentally unstable, and his love for your aunt is an obsession. People do rash things when they're possessed by obsessions. He's in there right now; he may have acted rashly if he thought we were going to take her away from him. The house told me to get us both out," she explained.

"Anyway, the police should be here soon, and they can work out what to do with him." Mary nodded at Lily.

A few minutes later, they heard the sirens before the police car arrived. A movement through the window of the top floor of Marion's house caught Lily's eye. She tried not to react, but Mary sensed something and looked up there, too.

Norman had worked out that he had been caught; he knew the police were on their way, he refused to be separated from Marion. No one was going to take her away from him or him away from her. It had always bothered Norman that Marion's wish to be cremated had been prevented by him, although he was sure she had forgiven him, and now, in the eleventh hour, he was going to give her the closest to it that he could with what he had available to him. He embraced Marion tightly to him as he doused them both with bottles of formaldehyde, he'd stolen from the morgue, pushed open the window and, with one smooth movement, set them alight and threw them both from it.

The police had arrived just in time to see the flaming bodies hit the ground. Initially, they had been suspicious of Lily and Mary's explanation, but their own investigation had proved it to be the truth.

Mary had eventually been given an urn with her Aunt Marion's properly cremated remains and been assured that there was none of Norman in there; Mary had her doubts but accepted them anyway. The police carried out extensive tests on the ashes from the original urn she'd been given and upon identifying them as the missing Morgue worker, Norman was ruled as his murderer, and they were returned to his family.

Norman was given a pauper's funeral and his ashes were never claimed."

Lily was shaking by the time she'd finished relaying the story to Hannah, the memory of Norman and his fiery death bringing back the original emotions she'd felt the day it had happened: a mixture of repulsion and disgust at his actions, tinged with the conflicting feeling of compassion for a boy who had been destroyed first by the abuses of his mother and then by his obsessions. And the memory of the nauseating stench of those two bodies burning, it had taken Lily weeks to feel she had washed that smell from her body, and it took a great deal of energy now to keep that memory from overpowering her with uncontrollable retching.

She had noticed, though, that that by the time she had finished telling Hannah the story, no trace of Norman or Marion seemed to remain.

Lily had been wrong; Norman hadn't become a powerful or malicious and hostile spirit; he had just remained trapped inside his obsession while his energy had slowly dwindled away. But with a retelling of his story and the knowledge that it was to become part of a more enduring form, the idea that he was to become lore allowed Norman's spirit to be off to wherever tormented souls like his went to repose and the memory of Marion was finally respectfully laid to rest.

"Please tell me there are not any stories scarier than this one," Hannah said when Lily had finished speaking.

"I can't really say if it's the scariest one because different things scare different people." Lily smiled. "It was the scariest one to me though. I've learnt through my gifts that, more often than not, it's the living that are scarier than the dead. I have tools that can protect me from the dead: amulets, crystals, silver jewellery, Wiccan blessings, things of that nature, but short of arming myself; I don't always know how to protect myself or someone else from a living evil," Lily reasoned, the fear that had been created in her by the events of Norman's story still evident, even all this time later.

"I'm sorry this story had such an effect on you, and now my questions are making it worse," Hannah apologised.

Lily fought to calm herself down, breathing deeply and soothing herself by running her hands over her clothes, smoothing imaginary wrinkles, composing herself before speaking again.

"No, it's okay, it's not your fault – I decided to tell you these stories, remember? It's not unusual to have a physical reaction to such a dark story – no need for you to apologise; it's really okay.

I'm okay now. How about we get out of here, and I'll take you home," Lily offered.

"Okay, just drop me off at my university. I think I'll hang out in the campus bar for a while to decompress before I go back to my room." She smiled, a bit embarrassed that she was scared.

"That sounds like a good idea," Lily told her and drove her to the university campus.

"Hannah, check your camera bag's front pocket," she said once they'd arrived.

"What? Okay." she agreed and checked the pocket. "What's this?" Hannah asked, holding the silver pendant she'd found.

"It's an evil eye amulet; it protects against evil spirits. I put it in there before we got out of the car; I just wanted you to have some protection if Norman tried anything." Lily smiled.

"Thank you so much." Hannah slipped the chain over her head. "It's beautiful. I've got three days off classes, so let me know when you're ready to do the next story." She smiled and got out of the car.

Lily watched her enter the campus bar before she drove away.

Chapter Three: The Empty Building

Two days after visiting White Pine Drive and recounting her time with Norman, Lily met Hannah at the gates of the Old Bellton Cemetery, leading her to the mysterious and forgotten building where their task for the day lay waiting.

"I bet you probably know every story in here, right?" Hannah asked, gesturing at the graves that sprawled before them, most of them hundreds of years old, many of them in various stages of decay and disarray – the people resting in them dead so long that they had no one left to care for them.

"I know some of them, but most of the bodies interred here don't have their spirits attached to them any more. In most cases, they've already moved on, though some of them are still dwelling in the places where they died. If there are any spirits here who need me to hear them so they can depart, I would hear them and come to listen." Lily smiled as Hannah stopped and produced a notebook to jot down what Lily had just told her before rushing to catch up with her.

"Where are we headed to?" Hannah asked Lily as she rejoined her.

"Just over there." Lily pointed past a row of graves up a hill that swelled behind a row of unkempt hedges. They walked in the direction Lily had indicated until the old building appeared before them.

"I didn't know this was here! Is this still the cemetery? Why is it empty except for this building?" Hannah blurted out, her eyes narrowing as she stared off into space, trying to figure out an explanation in her head.

"I've heard a lot of people say they don't know about this place; many of them don't even know where I'm talking about when I try to describe it. I've spent a great deal of time trying to find out who owns this building and if the ground it's on is still part of the graveyard, if it even has a name, but I've never been able to find any answers," Lily told her, a wistful note in her voice, leant by the sense of connection she felt to the building and the ground it stood on, from the years of dreams and hours spent investigating and all too little explanation in the scheme of things.

"So, how did you get this job?" Hannah asked, the idea having fixed on her that the answer to this might bring clues as to the ownership of the place and bringing out her phone; she started recording.

"I gave it to myself," Lily told her with a soft laugh. "Sorry, but there's no solution to the mystery of who owns the building or its land. Perhaps people sense that it's better to just leave it alone; that's what I thought when I first came here; the building is deserted; it has been empty for a very long time, but there's no graffiti, no sign of anyone having broken in and done the things inside that you would expect people to do to an empty and unwatched building. I think that anyone who comes near here, whether with intent to do harm or to take claim to sell or reside or perhaps demolish, is instead met with an ignorable sense of foreboding, something telling them that they should best be leaving it alone." Lily nodded to Hannah as she said this, convinced that her feeling was true.

"How about you? Did you feel that? Do you feel it now?" Hannah asked, wondering if they were welcome there.

"No, not at all; this place had been calling to me for a long time; it wanted me here so that I could hear its story so that I could tell it. And even though the spirits that were once here are now gone, the place itself will likely never be truly quiet or truly healed. A story like the one that unfolded here leaves an imprint, like a scar, the type of scar that will never fade. It's those scars that warn people away, that for all intents and purposes, hide this place from people; that's why its story needs to be in my book. That is why we're here today, Hannah," Lily explained.

"Well, I best be taking some photos so that you can tell me the story; the suspense is killing me!" Hannah admitted.

Lily nodded and let Hannah take a few establishing shots of the building's exterior as she walked up to the doors to see if they would let her in. Like they had all those years before, they swung open, welcoming her.

The building's bland exterior gave no clue to its purpose; a simple, double-story rectangle with a rusty gable roof, it contained four large portrait-orientated windows which had thick raw boards affixed in them in place of glass. It stood ominous and imposing, giving the impression that it was watching you, even though its window eyes were blind.

"Hannah, let's go in now to get a couple of pictures of the inside and then I'll tell you the story."

"Okay." Hannah obliged, and the two made their way around the dusty, discarded and broken things, with Lily indicating what to take pictures of.

When they were done, they went back outside, and the doors closed behind them.

"We better sit down; this is a pretty long story," Lily explained as the two sat on the old stone steps in front of the door. They did their best to find positions that were comfortable while

Lily told Hannah the following story as though she were a character in it.

"Lily grew up in a very old town with many of its own ghosts and stories to tell. Oftentimes, she needed to silence them, block out their whispers, just to be able to live there. It was so old that there were buildings that she couldn't find any information about in any books or archives, places with histories people had forgotten because anyone who had ever known them in the first place had long since died and been forgotten themselves. One of these buildings, empty and abandoned in a deserted section of an old graveyard, had for as long as Lily could remember, plagued her dreams. For most of her life, incessant reoccurring dreams, dark and most times scary, long dark hallways, screams and bangs, blood and crying, always mysterious with a nagging hangover-like effect that would follow her around begging to be solved. As Lily grew into a young adult, the dreams stopped for a time, but then, without warning or reason, they returned more ferocious and insistent than ever before. It was with the return of these dreams that she decided to solve the mystery for herself, her way.

The day had been temperate when Lily left home to go and find out the story inside the empty building, but on the way, grey clouds had begun to gather, making the day overcast and bringing a slight chill. By the time she'd arrived, the clouds were thick and black, turning the day almost night and the air bitingly cold.

The building stood tall and solitary, its once white exterior yellowed by hundreds of years of sun and neglect; Lily stood before the weathered doors, paint long since peeled, revealing rough raw timber and a well-rusted lock. She hadn't thought about how she was going to get inside, supposing her gift might be strong enough for the building's story to reveal itself to her through its walls. Besides, it had been calling to her for years; it wanted to tell her its story. This became evident as she took a step closer, the rusty lock disintegrating before her eyes as the doors swung menacingly open.

Lily had seen enough horror movies for her head to be telling her not to go inside, but this wasn't a horror movie and her need to know what the building's story was and stop the maddening dreams outweighed her uneasiness.

As she entered the building, she sensed something that she had never encountered before; it was cold and empty but pregnant with sorrow, so much sorrow, and rage and turmoil and malice. It was evil. Lily felt for her pouch of crystals in her pocket and found it safely there. She pulled her silver evil eye amulet up through the neck of her shirt, letting it hang on the outside, down the middle of her chest.

She looked around the large open room she'd entered into; there was a decaying couch and some broken chairs piled in a corner, scattered on the floor were some ageing and broken pieces of crockery covered with a thick film of dust, and by a doorway leading into a long hall was a pile of once white but now grey clothes, uniforms and hospital gowns the building told her. She could feel an abundance of energy circling her, the noise of hundreds of voices speaking over one another. She could not yet make out words, but she could sense their urgency. In her mind, Lily tried to communicate with them, telling them without words that she was there to help. She wanted to hear their stories but that she could only hear them if they spoke one at a time. It seemed then that an argument broke out amongst them, Lily heard a voice breakthrough, "I'm in charge here; I should get to go first!" Lily heard more than indignance in the shaking voice; it revealed someone who had been broken down to a whimpering fear and there too was what had existed before the breaking – a lack of kindness and compassion that bordered on evil.

"Oh, really flapdoodle, because being in charge went so well for you, why don't you shut up or you'll get some more!" a course blustering voice, bravado hiding not just fear but a lack of courage.

"Boys, boys, don't argue, or Gertrude will hear you; she'll tell Claudius and we'll all catch it!" Whimpering, afraid. In this one, too, Lily could hear more; there was loss and heartbreak, the heartbreak from the last lover in a long line of lovers to do her wrong, the one that sent her over the edge that she could never come back from – now she was lost, confused and broken, like a lost little girl.

"Bugger off hedge creeper, why don't you go gather some herbs for remembrance!" the coarse voice again; this time, Lily could hear the hate in it, hate born of fear for anyone that was different to him.

Lily tried for some time to get them to understand that she wanted their stories but needed them to go one at a time. All of a sudden, there was a loud scuffle followed by a slamming door and the turn of a key in a lock. It seemed that one of the voices had managed to force the others into a room and had locked them in there. Lily was now able to receive their stories one at a time.

*

The first one called himself Lamoak.

"I am Lamoak, son of Loki, with more evil intent and power than my father! I am not here for mischief but for torture; I am here to collect one thousand and one souls and then to collect one thousand and one more! I keep these souls from passing over, torturing them until they become so agonised that their agony turns to evil, that evil is powerful, so I will collect one thousand and one more and so on and so on until I have an all-powerful, omnipotent army to conquer every realm. You will bow down before me!" Lamoak's voice screamed in Lily's head louder than any other spirit before; it echoed inside her skull, threatening to split it open. She should have been terrified, but even as decaying chairs and old crockery began to fly around the room, no fear built in her.

Suddenly, she could see why; a scene played out in front of her, flickering and in sepia like a very old film:

A tall, painfully skinny man, his long dark hair flying madly about his sweaty face, cheekbones threatening to pierce through the pale skin pulled taught across them, was screaming like a banhe as he was dragged roughly inside by two burly men. They yelled at him harshly to stop screaming and each of them landed a punch on him when he did not comply, one on the side of his head and another in his stomach.

"I am King George IV. How dare you treat me in this manner? This is high treason! You will be hanged, drawn and quartered for this!" Spittle flew from his mouth as he became more enraged. More than outrage and the demand for respect and power, Lily could hear the depth of a deeply intelligent and artistically gifted man ravaged by a disease of the mind that he had lost control of. The men hit him again and he was wrestled into a straitjacket.

"I thought you were Loki's kid, King George; what happened there?" The slightly shorter of the two men laughed and kicked him before they dragged him down a hallway and threw him into a room. Lily could see inside the room; it was small with no windows; there was a lumpy mattress in the corner, soiled yellow and brown, with straw sticking from holes in numerous places all over it. The men threw a piece of mouldy bread at him before telling him that the doctor would see him tomorrow for bloodletting and then leaving him there, they locked the door behind them.

The man, now locked in what was essentially a cell, could hear screams issuing from other rooms in the building and cries echoing inside his own room that were not really there. He recoiled in horror at things that Lily couldn't see, though the building told her it was first snakes and then demons.

For what felt like hours, Lily was shown further scenes of this man, his hallucinations and paranoias growing with every minute. His mistreatment mounted with every day spent interred in what was, at that time, called Bellton Lunatic Asylum: bloodletting, freezing cold baths followed by roasting hot ones, beatings, days on end spent locked in his room with nothing.

He twice more tried to propel objects at her, a broken cup and another chair, she dodged both. And then he eventually showed her his death; Lily was expecting his demise to have come from a psychotic episode that resulted in him injuring himself so badly that he died or else a fatal beating from the asylum workers. The reality could have been attributed to a little of both; throughout his stay, the man whose true name was never known had many beatings and injured himself in fits of rage and psychosis many times. His wounds were never properly treated and like the other patients, he never had enough food to eat. He lived like a sick animal and eventually died from a culmination of all of his injuries, the malnutrition and the toll his illness had taken on his body, essentially dying of neglect. Lily watched as he failed to make it to his mattress one night, collapsing instead on the cold stone floor. Lily thought he had probably died before he hit the ground and the old building confirmed to her that this was the case.

Lily had doubted the existence of Lamoak from his initial self-introduction and now it was plain to see why, the spirit calling himself Lamoak was, in fact, the lost soul of a schizophrenic patient still trapped inside his worldly illness. Lily allowed herself to shed a few tears for this poor lost soul, assuring him that she would record his story and tell it so that he could now find his way home to rest.

She allowed herself a few moments before opening her mind up for the next one.

Next came to her a broken, childlike woman, small in stature; her long auburn hair flowed past her waist and was adorned with colourful flowers. She wore a long white dress that spoke of a different time; most of it was soiled and appeared dirty and tattered. She too appeared to Lily dangerously thin, though the previous story had taught her that if they didn't arrive that way, the conditions here would soon have them as such, her thinness though, further perpetuated her guileless childlike air.

"And will 'a not come again?

And will 'a not come again?

No, no, he is dead;

Go to thy deathbed;

He will never come again." She looked up towards Lily from a bowed head and then continued,

"His beard was as white as snow,

All flaxen was his poll.

He is gone; HE IS GONE.

And we cast away moan.

God 'a 'mercy on his soul!

And of all Christian souls, I pray to God. God, bye you." She turned and walked from the room, pausing in the hallway for a moment.

Lily recognised the speech from high school English; it was from 'Hamlet', spoken by Ophelia, and although this woman didn't seem to share the same madness as the man proclaiming to be King George IV and Lamoak, she did to seem to believe that she was Ophelia.

Ophelia soon re-entered the room carrying an arm full of flowers, always in character, the building told Lily.

"I didn't kill myself or drown by accident, you know!" Gone was the shaking, uncertain voice, and in its place was a woman bolstered by her convictions.

"Gertrude did it! She had knowledge that I had lain with Hamlet and that I was heavy with child.

"She tried to influence me to end my life by confiding in me that she had been laying with my father for many years and that he was most likely Hamlet's true father! This reprehensible news made pity in me, it's true, though before I was able to devise of any action, Gertrude saw the folly in telling me her secret and sought to mend her troubles.

"Hiding behind the willow, askant the brook she sat in wait for my arrival. There, she had already gathered a heavy bundle of flowers and so too had woven a crownet of others for mine head. When I approached from behind, she hit me with a heavy rod concealed in her dresses. As I fell, she pushed the heavy bundle into my arms and hastily the crownet on my head; in my scramble to right my posture, she pushed me hard into the brook and at last, her intent was found; she watched me, chanting snatches of old lauds as I floundered and my garments grew heavy with their drink and pulled me to my muddy death." She sighed as she finished telling her story, as though the weight of retelling it tired her out.

"Of course, these vazey dizzards here don't believe me, but their opinions mean nought to me!"

She stopped speaking then and sat on the ground in front of Lily. The words between them stopped, and instead, like the sepia-toned flickering movie projected by Lamoak, images began to play straight into her mind.

At first, the scene matched the one she had described, down to the period costumes, but as it progressed, a new scene broke through and it became painfully clear to Lily that although the woman before her had long ago embraced a reality where she was a Shakespearian character living inside one of his most famous plays so completely that she was absolutely and completely Ophelia, daughter of Polonius, sister of Laertes, lover of Hamlet, it may actually have been her steadfast belief of this that led to her ultimate demise.

The scene that broke through, running first on top of and then in place of the scene Ophelia had described, was taking place inside the building they were now in, the Bellton Lunatic asylum some two hundred or more years ago and it was not Queen Gertrude who had drowned Ophelia; it was the arguing voices from earlier. Lily watched in horror as three men, one of them Lamoak, pushed Ophelia back and forth between them, sniping barbs about herbs and flowers, her dead father and 'that dandy, Hamlet'. She grew more distressed with each slap, both physical and verbal, until they began threatening her,

"Give up the act, or we'll drown you ourselves!" Lily watched as Ophelia refused to say she was not who she was – for it was not a lie; in her mind, she truly was Ophelia Living inside Elsinore. Two of the men backed off, letting her go, but they remained in the room to watch and jeer, keeping lookout as the man who remained hold of her raped and then drowned her in the bathtub.

"Did you see, did you see how Gertrude drowned me?" Ophelia asked Lily in clear distress.

"Yes, Ophelia, I did, and I'm so sorry, but now your story has been told and I will keep it for you. I will tell it to others so that you may have justice. And with that, you may finally rest." Lily could feel that even in her final moments, the woman who was Ophelia kept herself safe inside her sanctuary of being Ophelia; she was not raped by a dirty and depraved asylum worker while two other patients watched; she was not drowned in a dirty bathtub in a rat-infested asylum. She was, of course, drowned in a brook by the queen, surrounded by flowers and looking like an ethereal mermaid. There was no point in disputing her narrative because her mind had experienced no other, and it was of no help in getting her spirit to rest.

Lily had noticed the slight deviation from the true narrative of 'Hamlet', though she could recall some lively debate in her English classroom about this Ophelia's description of events being what had really occurred. She wondered if this Ophelia had encountered such scholarly debate herself, though she doubted it; her being a female in the time that she had been, her attendance at school or university was unlikely. Instead, Lily thought to herself, and the building confirmed to her that for some time, this woman's reality had been the plot of Hamlet and in her final moments, being violated and murdered, a further splinter occurred, creating an alternate version of the storyline that now better suited her narrative and better insulated her from the unbearable truth of her reality.

Artists had rendered paintings of the death of Ophelia and poets had composed ballads in her honour; Lily thought this was a much nicer death than this Ophelia had really had, and she was glad that she was safe inside her illusion.

Lily wept for Ophelia as she faded from her vision and steeled herself for the next one.

Lily was not surprised when the next spirit to approach her with his story was the one she'd just watched drown Ophelia. He was the first one to have spoken to her, indignant with the others not obeying him. She had already sensed evil in him, but he was working hard for her to believe otherwise. Before her stood a young man, angular in a uniform that hung from him, fresh-faced and eager to please; he projected images of himself being kind to the asylum's inmates, feeding them carefully, bathing them lovingly, patting their heads or backs, helping them drift off to sleep and attending them faithfully when their paranoias and insanities became too much, speaking to them in low and cooing voices, reasoning with them until they felt calm and safe. These images soon faltered; the spirit had spent too much of his energy projecting a lie and the other spirits still available of any energy were combining theirs with the energy of the building itself to tear down the deceiving visions so that Lily could see the truth.

The skinny, kind man faltered, and now before her stood a large man, bloated by his position of power; he was dirty and fat from eating the dinners of others and from the satiety he obtained from tormenting those he was tasked to care for. The true story attached to this spirit was sinister; it showed asylum inmates going hungry for days whilst Roy, as Lily soon learned was his name, first wolfed down their meals and then told them they had already eaten them themselves. He would then tell the same to the two other workers if they bothered to ask and it was only rare that they did, for although they weren't malicious like Roy, they cared less about the inmates than the job itself. The Doctor,

Victor, who was lucky to have visited once a month, cared even less about any of it, except for the laudanum.

The asylum would receive a quarterly parcel from England that contained three months' worth of laudanum. Lily watched as Roy would take a few days' worth and add it to so much water that he had a dose for each inmate for a few months. The rest he'd secret away, taking some of it himself; He'd seclude himself in an empty room or else kick the inhabitants out fiercely. Once alone, Lily watched him drink some himself, becoming slow and languid, slumping against a wall or on one of the inmate's mattresses, his face wearing a look of stupefied euphoria. The rest of the package would go to Dr Victor, who would exchange with Roy a large number of coins in a leather purse for the bottles wrapped discreetly in newspaper.

Any inmates who struck the courage to dare to question the strength or the lack of effect felt from their medicine were sometimes given another dose of water, but mostly, they were slapped, kicked or thrown against a wall.

A very vivid montage began to play for Lily in which she watched as patients were slapped and pinched. Instead of their paranoias being soothed, they were fed.

In one instance, a woman who had escaped a very abusive husband, committed for hysteria, was plagued with the fear of him coming to kill her, regularly Roy would tell her that he'd seen him outside or that Dr Victor had organised for her husband to come and take her home the next day. On occasion, he'd even pretend that he was her husband and he'd chase her around until she was screaming and sobbing, almost choking on her own wracking breaths.

Another of Roy's favourite pastimes was to plague a particular young girl who was driven to madness by her empathy for the Indigenous people of the land. She had only a few years prior been living in close proximity to a camp of local Aboriginal people, befriending many of them. She had spent many hours in their company learning their ways and even playing games with their children. She was awoken very early one morning, so early that she was not sure if it was morning or night, so dark was it still. She heard horses galloping past her house towards the Aboriginal camp; then she heard a child's cry, some shouting, a great commotion, and many gunshots. She stayed in her home terrified and when she eventually managed to gain the courage to venture outside, she found the campground empty, though marred with clear signs of a struggle, with all their humpies destroyed and much blood staining the ground. She never saw any of her friends again.

Roy loved to tell her stories in great detail about how her friends had been killed and the few survivors dragged away to prisons. Although the stories Roy was telling her were not lies, there was no need for the greatly embellished detail and the joy he took in telling her so callously. He also liked to insist to her that it was her kindness to the Dharwal tribe and her consorting with them had led to their capture. This woman was so disturbed by the images Roy forced into her mind that she stopped eating and drinking and took to her bed; there, she became thinner and thinner until she was little more than skin and bones. Eventually, she was so weak, her energy stores being completely depleted, that she could no longer rise from her bed nor move at all. In the end, her hair fell out; her bones protruded so that they threatened to tear through her now paper-thin skin. In the final stages of starvation, she hallucinated horrible pictures of the stories Roy had told her about her friends, but so weak by now was she that she could no longer cry or speak at all. Soon, an infection ravaged what little was left of her and after three agonising months, she had starved to death. Lily could not sense a strong presence of her spirit; she suspected that there was only enough left for her to show her what had sent her declining into madness and what Roy had done to her.

After years of Roy's torment, with numerous patients perishing due to his actions, and even one at his own hand, a rebellion grew, eventually manifesting into a mutiny. The inmates gathered their last vestiges of reason and any lingering remnants of sanity to band together and hatch a plan. Once a month, there was a day when Roy was the only worker at the asylum. This was usually a dreaded day, but this one particular time, it was a godsend. Lamoak, though likely psychotic and definitely insane, was a great planner and an even better leader. He assembled a crew of seven inmates, though his plan could be carried out on his own, the others insisted on helping; they all wanted Roy to know how hated he was.

Lamoak had seen where Roy hid the Laudanum that he sold to the doctor, and the previous night, he had removed all of it from its hiding place after Roy had fallen asleep in his office. Roy had conveniently more passed out than fallen asleep after a night of heavy drinking. The inmates knew from years of his antics that upon arising with a hellish hangover, he would immediately reach for more whiskey, for hair of the dog. With this in mind, Lamoak emptied the entire stash of laudanum into the bottle beside Roy. All that next morning, the inmates kept quiet, entertaining themselves with silent games and hushed activities. When they finally heard him stirring in the early afternoon, the prepared seven hastened to his office to say their piece to him.

Roy sat up in shock to see them so brazenly enter his domain but attended first to the more important task of drinking his whiskey to still the roar of his head and abate the rush of nausea in his stomach. He'd deal with them later, and harshly, he smiled to himself.

The seven circled him as he drank down his poisoned whiskey; they did not need to wait long for the massive dose of laudanum to take effect. They watched as he tried to struggle against the strength of the opiate sleep; trying to form curses against them, he slumped to the ground.

The group began taunting him.

"Gibface!" shouted one.

"You're a disgusting hornswoggler!" Spat another.

"You great bumbling jollocks!" One kicked him.

Roy listed sideways and looked up at them in confusion as he began having trouble breathing.

"You, Roy, are a pigeon-livered meater and we've had enough of your buggery. Today is the day you get what you deserve!" Lamoak told him firmly.

The seven began slapping and kicking him; they moved about him in a circle, pinching and twisting his skin until he began to beg them to stop. Instead, they laughed at him.

It became harder and harder for Roy to breathe; a heavy tiredness was creeping over him. The inmates were unsure if he was scared, but they hoped he was. When he had turned blue and there was scarcely a breath being drawn by him any more, Lamoak kicked him once more so that he sprawled face down. He turned to the others, and they nodded in agreement and left the room so that Roy would die alone.

And die he did; the whole event took an hour from beginning to end and the last fifteen minutes he spent pissing and shitting himself as he slowly suffocated to death alone. A lenient punishment for the years of anguish he'd caused.

As the image of a finally dead Roy flickered and faded away, a tired Lily sat on the dusty stone floor. Without words heard by her, even in her mind and without images seen, she instead attained knowledge from feelings, A flotilla of sensations and emotions imparted to her, left over from the spent energy of the spirits who'd faded over the last two hundred years and the life of the building itself; melancholy, psychosis, depression, anxiety, wroth, injustice, hysteria, mourning, heartbreak, trauma, suicide, murder and deceit. The building and those within it had experienced them all.

It took Lily an hour to summon enough energy to pick herself up from the floor; she left the decrepit building and very slowly made her way home, the sorrow and sadness slowing her down as it weighed on her. Lily had solved the mystery of the empty building for herself. That night, she dreamed once more of the haunting lunatic asylum, but this time, it was not scary or sad; her dream was of a procession of lost souls being found; they drifted away from that place of imprisonment and sorrow, their mystery solved, and their stories told, they were finally able to rest.

Lily never dreamed of the old building again, but she thought of the inmates from time to time as one would an old friend."

"Wow, that is a crazy, amazing story." Hannah exhaled. "Sorry, not crazy, like lunatic, I didn't mean…" she tapered off, not knowing what to say.

"That's okay, it *is* pretty crazy, and some of them *were* lunatics, well that's what they called it back then, but some of them were just sad and used up, some of them had too much empathy for the world they lived in and some of them were maybe just evil or made evil by things that had happened to them.

But they're all at peace now," Lily said, reminding Hannah that they had been set free by telling her their story.

"Are you okay?" Hannah asked Lily, noticing the melancholy lilt to her voice.

"Yeah, I'm okay; it's like watching a sad movie where all the characters are your friends. I feel so connected to all of the poor souls who lived and died here. I dreamed about this place so many times, for so many years and though I never saw their faces, it was them I was dreaming of. Those dreams had become a part of me, so when their story set them free, and I stopped dreaming of them, it felt as though I lost a part of myself, like losing an old friend, but the memory remains," Lily explained.

"I can't stay sad, though, because they're all at peace now. And that's the point of it all, of every story I am told," She reminded Hannah.

"Yes, of course," Hannah replied, understanding the attachment Lily felt to the spirits and their stories and acknowledging that the point of them was to give them peace.

She turned off the recording and put her phone away as the two stretched their protesting muscles, which were now cramped and aching from hours of sitting on hard stone. Goodbyes were exchanged and arrangements made for the next visit of their project.

Chapter Four: The Fortune Teller: Madame Zelda/Madame Marnie

Natalie Edgar had no special powers, she had no gift of foresight, she was not a medium or a channeler and she certainly was not a conduit to the dead. She did, however, claim to be all of these things and it was at least one, if not all of them, that led to her untimely death.

When she was claiming to be a fortune teller, she called herself the very familiar 'Madame Zelda', thinking it lent to her credibility by sounding authentic. When she was professing to be a medium with many channels to reach the dead, she called herself, for reasons unknown, 'Madame Marnie'. Lily was not sure if it was Zelda or Marnie that got Natalie killed, ultimately resulting in the death of all three of them, but seeing as that Natalie had been all three of them, it seemed only fair that the blame lay with her rather than her fictitious personas.

The fortune teller, as Lily called her, had been one of her earliest jobs. She'd received an email and then a phone call from a woman who'd heard strange stories about the person who'd lived in her house before her. She had explained to Lily that their house had sat empty for many years before they'd moved in and now she and her family were experiencing some unusual activity in the home; at first, it was doors and drawers opening and closing by themselves and lights that flickered on and off, now however, the occurrences felt more sinister, with candles blowing out by themselves, and the temperature dropping, often paired with the smell of incense and the distinct feeling of someone having just left the room. The Lutts family was scared and was looking for answers.

Two days later, Lily arrived at the Lutts's home to find them some answers and twenty years later she went back there with Hannah to tell her the story.

*

"Kathy Lutts was sitting outside waiting for me when I got here," Lily told Hannah as they arrived at 112 Ocean Avenue Evilly Vale.

"She was more afraid than when we'd spoken earlier on the phone because whatever it was that was in the house was now appearing to her young son, Christopher," Lily explained. She looked out the car window at the house; it was dilapidated, but more than that, she thought to herself, the house looked like it had been broken down by too many years of sadness, too much sadness, and regret, so much regret, and so much sorrow and fear. It had long been standing empty, Lily was sure, but as she looked up at the two quarter-moon windows, looking back at her like eyes from behind the boards that had been nailed across them, she glimpsed some movement. Lily sensed something faintly familiar, like the unknown energy she'd felt twenty years prior; only now it had grown stronger. Lily knew there was another story here for her, a newer one, one that had not yet occurred in its entirety when last she was there. In her head, she quietly asked for it to wait for her. In the window, the movement she had seen took a wispy form and nodded yes.

"I think it's best I tell you the story from here before we go up to the house," Lily informed Hannah, trying to keep her voice light and discreetly opening her door a crack to drop her clear quartz crystal outside the car.

"Yeah, okay, whatever's best for you," Hannah agreed, sensing that Lily was discerning something she hadn't expected but leaving it for Lily to explain later; she got her phone ready to record Lily's story from twenty years before.

With a slight nod of her head, Lilly indicated to Hannah that she was ready to start. Pressing record on her phone, Hannah settled back to listen to the tale in its entirety, being familiar enough with Lily now to know that she would anticipate any questions and answer them to the best that the spirits allowed without needing to be asked.

"I could feel her as soon as I mounted the steps. Natalie Edgar was sad and angry for a whole host of reasons, but her energy was waning; she would soon cease to exist as an entity, so I assured Kathy that her home would soon be disturbance free, and her son would soon stop being kept awake at night by ghostly apparitions.

Asking if I minded if she waited outside, Kathy lit a cigarette as I told her I'd be fine on my own. When I entered the house, I was struck by a different energy, one that wasn't entirely Natalie. It was panicky and agitated; I could feel it sliding into hysteria, but that's all it was, a feeling; it wasn't a presence, it wasn't a second spirit and it wasn't giving me a story, just a hint that there was something else there. I didn't tell Kathy about it because I couldn't define it and I didn't want to add to her fear. I thought it would probably disappear along with Natalie, so I put it out of my mind. I moved into the living room, where I could feel Natalie without the interference of the disquieting energy and that's where I heard Natalie's story. It played out almost instantly in my mind; seventy-some years' worth of pain, anger, hate and revenge became known to me.

It was 1930, and Natalie Edgar was nine when her father died; that on its own was bad enough, but it wasn't on its own; his death marked her mother's descent into a madness that dragged them both down, first to poverty, then to pariahdom and eventually to hell. It was six long years before her mother joined her father in the ground, but it would have been much better for everyone involved if she had just died with him that same day. His death had come sudden and instant from an accident at the building site he worked on; he felt no pain, he did not suffer. Natalie's mother, by contrast, suffered from the moment she got the news that he was dead and her dying lasted those full six years before her pain finally ended. Natalie's pain had many more years to endure.

Natalie and her mother weren't plunged into immediate poverty upon the death of her father, but the loss of his income did make them poor. There was a meagre amount of savings that her mother initially refused to touch, instead taking in sewing and ironing to supplement the scant wage she earned from cleaning people's homes. This saw the end of Natalie's dancing lessons and removed without question any hope of new things or her attendance to school excursions, outings with friends or birthday parties. With her clothes worn and unfashionable and her possessions lacking any accoutrements of the latest fads, the sympathy her friends had initially felt for her over the death of her father soon turned to pity and then, more quickly, to disdain. And with her absence from all things social, her presence at school at first became awkward, and as the pity and disdain turned to spurning, it became unbearable.

Over this time, as Natalie became a sad outcast, her mother had at first not noticed, but then when it became obvious, she ignored it, and so deep was she in her grief over her husband's death, she did not care. She was bewitched by the idea of contacting her husband, refusing to believe that he was gone, not questioning as to whether he had gone to heaven or hell, but believing that he was waiting around in spirit form to be contacted by her. She thought that if they could communicate one last time, that the heavy shadow of grief would be lifted from her and that, somehow, everything would be all right. She became obsessed with this idea, preoccupied by it to the cost of all else, spending hours in the library searching for ways to speak with the dead, until a circus came to town, bringing with it a fortune teller.

The fortune teller spent many hours with Natalie's mother, taking her money and telling her little of truth but feeding her enough of the things she wanted to hear to keep her coming back for more. The fortune teller agreed with Natalie's mother that her husband was still around, telling her that his spirit was restless and did indeed need to speak to her one last time before he could rest. The day that the circus was leaving town, the fortune teller told Natalie's mother all about mediums and how speaking to one of them or attending a séance was her best, nay her only hope, for ever speaking to her husband and allowing him to rest in peace. That week spent with the fortune teller led to the proverbial cupboards being bare. Subsequently, over the next week, Natalie and her mother went without dinner for three days and then any food at all for two more. Her Mother kept steadfast in her refusal to touch their paltry nest egg. Natalie suspected, with bitterness growing inside her along with the hunger, that her mother was saving this money for the ridiculous expenditure of engaging a medium.

Even as her mother returned to her cleaning work and took

in more mending and ironing, the cupboards remained mostly bare, stocked scantily with only the barest of essentials in the smallest quantities possible. For Natalie was right, her mother was fixated on the notion of engaging a medium to conduct a séance and when she had finally found one two hours away in the city, they had told her that she was likely going to need more than one séance to reach her husband and that each was going to be very costly.

Aside to this, as the town began to gossip about the Edgar family, her mother was offered less and less mending and ironing and one by one, the houses that needed cleaning began to drop off. The gossip was brewed from Mrs Edgar's erratic behaviour and dishevelled appearance around town and worse than that, she was constantly rambling about speaking to her dead husband and even worse than that still, she had taken to drink. Natalie's mother was now a drunkard slipping into insanity and very publicly, too.

She ambled around town, bottle in brown paper bag, fooling no one. Taking trains to and fro the city to hand over money she could ill afford, to be lied to by a woman with no ability to commune with the dead at all. All the while, believing that the money she was parting with was helping that con woman to grow her husband's spirit strong so that he could appear to her for them to speak.

Meanwhile, Natalie's sadness grew, so did her bitterness and slowly but surely, her respect for her mother began to slip away, as did her attendance at school, and being as that it was a spiteful, hurtful place to be, she stopped going, she was barely twelve. And seeing as her presence had become a burden, with the other children constantly picking on and fighting with her, the teachers trying to pretend that she didn't smell or not notice that she had no lunch again, no one asked where she was when she stopped attending altogether.

This gave Natalie long, lonely days to brood over her mother's actions, the lack of respect blossoming into her realisation that her mother was acting like an idiot. She could hardly blame the town for ostracising her mother, but she did blame her mother for them ostracising her. However, her mother, the Bernice Edgar that Natalie had known before her father had died, was gone, replaced by a stupid woman, weak and ineffectual, dumb enough to be taken in by charlatans and too drunk to pull herself out of her grief. Her slide into insanity now complete.

These three years gone had hardened Natalie; instead of feeling empathy for her mother over their shared loss, she grew to hate the woman and the man who had caused it all. When finally, the work completely dried up for Bernice, she eventually, with no other choice, began using the modest savings that had been set aside.

Natalie's mother had convinced her to go to the medium with her, but one time, that once was enough for Natalie to cement in her mind what she already knew, that her mother was an idiot being taken for a ride, as were the many other people handing over their hard-earned money for parlour tricks. But no amount of pleading or reasoning with her mother would make her see sense; in the end, Natalie gave up, hoping that eventually she would be tricked into thinking she'd gotten what she needed and then maybe all of this would go away, she was beyond caring if the Bernice she knew ever came back to her as a mother.

Natalie presumed that the medium fleecing her mother would have continued to do so had she not drunk herself to death three years later. By this time, the savings had, of course, all been spent, and it had been a year or more since anyone had offered her mother work; she was too ravished by her grief and her inebriation, too far in insanity now, even if they had. Natalie had been forced to fend for them both; unfortunately, it soon became painfully clear that Natalie was not very good at anything, and so, for a time, she turned tricks. Upon returning home from this one night, she found her mother face down in a pile of her own vomit; on closer inspection, she found that she was dead.

Being as that she wasn't really any much better at turning tricks than at any of the other things she'd tried her hand at to make a living, a plan that to some, perhaps upon hearing her story would seem obvious, began to hatch in her mind.

She had seen the medium her mother had gone to; she knew how she dressed, the theatrical property strewn about her and the eccentricities she affected; she also knew from her mother's excited ramblings how the fortune teller at the circus had presented herself, the words she had used and the affectations in her use. With this forefront in her mind, Natalie gathered what she needed: costumes featuring head scarves, shawls and robes, hoop earrings, decks of well-worn tarot cards, crystal necklaces and anything that might lend itself to being mystical. Some she thrifted, some she stole while they were flapping in the wind, drying on people's clotheslines. Then she remembered a great trick her mother had taught her, though painfully embarrassing at the time, at first, she fought against the memory in her mind, but then she became thankful for its welcome lesson – it had been a particularly cold winter in the third year after her father's death, with their money all but gone, Natalie's clothes had either warn out or grown too small, and Bernice had only one warm coat, so there was none to lend a shivering Natalie. And so, out of desperation, was born a plan, necessity being the mother of *invention; her mother went over and over the plan with her with her before they entered the diner. It was blistering outside, so although Natalie did not want to lie to the nice old lady who worked at the diner, she was happy to go in out of the weather.*

"Hello, this one was in yesterday with my pa and they left her coat behind," her mother said, pushing Natalie forward. "It'll be the last time I let those two out together, her off with her daydreams about some boy and him off with the fairies; they'll leave their heads behind next time," she said to the woman behind the counter, the name tag pinned above her ample breast read, 'Vera'.

"Of course, let me get the lost and found box for you, dear," Vera said. She knew who Bernice was and doubted the story to be true, but the winter wasn't even half over and if Natalie Edgar didn't get a coat, she'd likely die of pneumonia before the spring came. Vera put the box on the counter and left them to rummage through it. Natalie had gotten two coats, a scarf, a woollen hat and a pair of gloves that day. Natalie's embarrassment and objections to lying soon disappeared when her body was no longer aching with cold.

And once she'd remembered this trick her mother had devised, she soon had the rest of the paraphernalia she required to earn some money for herself and to get some justice for the fleecing that had been done to her mother. The money she took from people as Madame Zelda and Madame Marnie was owed to her, she told herself. And people who were stupid, believing in things mystical and occult, like her mother, deserved to be parted from their money.

It never dawned on her, not until after her life had been taken from her for doing it, that all she was really doing was taking advantage of people's pain and doing to other people what had been done to her mother and by extension, to her. By the time that realisation came, it was too late; the damage had been done and she had paid the ultimate price.

For around twenty years, she swindled people; she was never caught, for it was hard to disprove her claims when she never promised anything except her attempt to see the future or her attempt to speak with your dead loved one. Any fortunes not come true were out of her hands and at the fault of the gods or destiny. And no proof could be made of the inauthenticity of communications with the dead; it wasn't a science, after all. Natalie made herself much money, much more than her mother had ever lost, but through sheer quantity; she did much more damage to innocent, lost, grieving people than had ever been done to her and her mother.

She first perfected her fortune teller act before promoting herself to medium. The fortune telling came easy enough; her formula consisted of mostly telling people things they wanted to hear, as most of them were universal, and with a little divining from their appearance or a look in their eye, she soon made herself a reliable menu of fortunes to be told. A woman looking lost and sad, either thin or fat, would be told that she was worthy and deserving of love and that she would soon find the one; Zelda could feel him getting closer. A man with unironed clothes, a three-day growth, with or without the obvious signs of a hangover, could always be satisfied by some variation of – you're going to get that job/ the next job will be the one and/or your wife is going to come to her senses and come back to you, I'm almost sure of it.

If it seemed these didn't apply, she'd switch to her other method, letting the customer, or rube as she silently called them, prattle on about their problems and their woes; in this way, she *could predict the thing to tell them which would satisfy them best.*

Then came a day that she needed not to use her menu or her listening skills, nor were true fortune-telling skills needed; the day Patricia Williams walked into her tent at the annual fisher fair.

Patricia struggled to hide her protruding belly, slight but obvious on her skinny frame, trying to keep it hidden under layers of coats as she wobbled over the uneven dirt terrain of the fairground. She kept looking back over her shoulder, hoping no one was recognising her visiting a fortune teller and, worse still, that no one was recognising her as the underage, unwed woman bringing shame on herself and her family.

"Yes, come in. "Madame Zelda rose to help Patricia in, zipping the door flap of the tent shut behind her and assisting her into a chair.

"Hello, I— my name is Pa—"

"Patricia," Madame Zelda finished for her, for although Patricia had quickly and with relief, forgotten Natalie's face when she had left school, Natalie remembered her. She was one of the many children who had pitied and then hated her, but for the first and perhaps the only time in her long, misguided search for justice for her mother and herself, Natalie felt compassion for the person in front of her.

"Oh, of course you know my name, silly me!" Patricia admonished herself – of course, a clairvoyant would know her name.

"Yes." Madame Zelda smiled as she nodded at her and stopped Patricia from providing her with her story, as enough of it was obvious she didn't need to be told what Patricia wanted her fortune to focus on.

"You find yourself in trouble. You've kept it a secret until

now, but you are no longer able to conceal it and you do not know what to do. You are scared." Madame Zelda had, over time, developed a slight accent, faintly Russian, that Natalie believed lent authenticity to her act. She paused. As Patricia nodded, holding back tears.

"You were lied to; you were in love, the boy—" Natalie caught the look in Patricia's eye and corrected, "The man told you he loved you, he promised he was going to marry you and now he will not." She demurred from using the harsher and more definite 'refused'; refraining from definitive was an important tool for Madame Zelda to never be wrong.

Patricia was nodding. "I just don't know what to do. Can you tell me what's going to happen to me?" she pleaded, her eyes wide and her chest rising and falling in anxious breaths.

"I can; it will be hard to hear, and I'm sorry for it, but it is better you be aware of the truth so that you can make the right decisions, the right decisions for yourself and for the baby." Natalie placed her hand on Patricia's as Madame Zelda, but she didn't need to be Madame Zelda to predict the bleak future Patricia would have in 1938 if she insisted on having her baby unwed, even if she did 'go to the country' and have the nuns give it to a waiting family – she knew what it was to be a pariah and be driven to vice and insanity from it and the poverty. There was an alternative, a much easier secret to keep and without the life of both Patricia and a child being ruined, Natalie believed it the best option.

"Patricia, if you carry this baby to term, whether you keep it or let it be given away, you will be shunned by your family and friends, as will the child; you will be eschewed from society and plunged into ruin. I can feel cold and loneliness, hunger, pain, sickness, death and sorrow for all involved. Especially the child," Madame Zelda said with a gentle tone.

"What can I do?" Patricia's tears flowed now, her heartbreak and fear writ all over her face.

"There is only one option; it might scare you. You may think it is wrong, but I can assure you that it is not wrong. You will be safe; it will take only a little while. You will stay in recovery for a few hours, and then you will go on your way. Your life will be restored, your happy future reinstated." Madame Zelda fished a card from her robes and slid it across the table to the weeping woman.

"I know many women who have seen this doctor: rich women, poor women, married women, young women, older women, and women exactly like you. She is qualified and experienced, she is careful and caring, she is discreet, and she is your salvation. You must go to her," Madame Zelda told her. She knew the doctor would take care of Patricia; many of the women she travelled with, in the fairs and carnivals, the circuses and shows had used her for her same services, and they were all living and continuing lives that would otherwise have been ruined in the conservative patriarchy of the day.

"You may have heard people say uninformed, terrible things about people who see such doctors, but you pay them no heed. I can tell you with a certainty that no mark is made on your soul from such a choice and the..." Madame Zelda nodded at Patricia's stomach and continued, "never was, the soul it was to be simply returns to heaven and waits for another baby to be born into, it will not be hurt and it will not wait very long." Madame Zelda assured her. Natalie did not believe a word she had said about the baby's soul; it was said only to serve Patricia's needs – whether she believed it or not did not matter as long as it helped her feel better about it and make the right decision.

Patricia looked at the card and with tears drying, seemed to accept, if not welcome, her fate. She had already been considering such an alternative but was faltering in its ethics. Now, reassured by Madame Zelda, who seemed so wise, she saw it as the only alternative.

"Don't worry about paying me for today; you can use that money for the doctor. Just ring her to make an appointment, or you can go to the address on the card and she'll tell you when she can fit you in." It was the one good deed Natalie ever did and the truest reading Madame Zelda ever gave.

The two said their goodbyes and wished each other well.

Natalie believed without a doubt that it was a good deed she performed that day. You did not need to be clairvoyant to predict what would, without a doubt, have been Patricia's fate if she had birthed her unwanted child, but unfortunately for Natalie, her one good deed could not undo all the bad she had done and continued to do after that day, the bad that wrote her karma for her and cemented her ultimate fate.

Soon after this day, Natalie decided to give up the fortune telling and focus more on being a medium; she believed that her fortune teller act, now being perfected, gave her the experience she needed to move on to the more lucrative act of channelling the dead. She also didn't care to find herself accidentally caring for anyone and had confidence that she was less likely find any compassion for people who, to her, were just like her weak and feeble-minded mother.

In establishing herself as a medium, she decided to give up travelling with the fairs and circuses, believing that setting herself up in one place gave her services more credibility than those procured from a medium in a travelling show. She found herself a perfect establishment, a large house that looked appealing but not imposing, with a large room just off the entry, perfect for hosting her customers for her act.

She called the room her parlour and decorated it with a large tapestry depicting the phases of the moon and another displaying the zodiac chart. She set up shelves along one wall to house books on the occult, mysticism and spirituality, adding strategically placed ornaments of crystals and candles. In the centre of the room was a large table with a crystal ball off to one side and a candelabrum on the other. She had a trunk full of other props, chosen depending upon the nature of the client; it contained crucifixes, bibles, rosary beads, statues and pictures of various saints, bunches of sage and other herbs, and a whole array of things she had either seen in the house of the medium her mother had dragged her to, or come across in books about the craft – both the true craft of mediumship and the craft of conning at it. And with a carefully crafted set up of fishing line and magnets, learned from her conning books, Madame Marnie was able to move curtains, the tapestries and objects at times most opportune to her acts, and with precisely trimmed candle wicks she could have a candle's flame seem to blow out after precisely seven seconds, a very convincing accoutrement to her shows.

Once she'd furnished and rigged her parlour appropriately, she commissioned a large sign to be made for her to hang in front of the house, just behind the low picket fence, next to the gate. It read in large and ornate letters: Madame Marnie, Medium and Channeler.

But Natalie did not simply sit and wait for the sign to bring in business, for that left too much to chance; she didn't care for the generic mediations she could perform from the scant information elicited from someone coming in off the street.

Instead, she spent hours each morning scouring the obituaries and funeral notices in the newspapers, finding potential marks. Armed with the information given there, she was able to devise a somewhat less generic and more convincing mediation, soon developing a menu similar to the one she'd used as a fortune teller. For the parent grieving the loss of a child, it was always safe to say that the child says they love you, they're sorry they had to go, don't be sad, they're not in pain any more. The loss of a spouse was usually addressed with similar words, but Natalie knew that to build her reputation and gain more clients through recommendations, she needed to know much more about the deceased before the grieving mother, father, husband, wife, friend, son, daughter, etc. walked in her door. Thinking on this is where Natalie stumbled across the idea of going to the funerals that she read about in the papers, there she could hide in the back and garner information on the dead, their passions and achievements usually listed, a synopsis of their life likely given and often there was a large picture of them allowing Madame Marnie to develop a much more personalised and convincing experience of channelling their spirit. It was also financially beneficial for her to approach whomever of the mourners was most likely to be seeking closure or one final meeting with the departed, easy enough for her to pick out; it was usually the one crying the most, looking the most lost, or the most inconsolable. Natalie, who had never been much good at anything in her life, became very good at sensing how much someone's grief was worth to her and even better at exploiting that grief to line her pockets handsomely. Approaching these mourners, she would tell them that their loved one was still present, that they could not pass over and find peace until they spoke to them one more time- of course, for a fee, she can perform that service for them, adding that it is the only way they'll be able to communicate with the spirit and the only way their loved one will find their peace. It worked ridiculously well, making Natalie a professional at taking advantage of grief and Madame Marnie a revered channeler of the dead.

What Natalie did not know, because she possessed no real powers of psychic ability and understood little of the realm she was disrespecting, was that her fraudulent and callous acts were building up against her, her karma being irrevocably damaged, and the anger of the supernatural realm was growing into something tangible and finally that anger was realised in the only true spirit that Natalie ever encountered, the recently deceased husband of her last client.

Harold Ferguson died a sudden death; five days prior to his funeral, he was ripped from life when the tram he was riding home from work collided with a bus being driven by an inexperienced driver, he was killed instantly. His wife Madeleine was predictably inconsolable; the shock had threatened to kill her, and she had, in fact, spent three days in hospital having her heart and blood pressure monitored after she had collapsed and been unable to stop weeping. Eventually, a sense of duty took over and she sternly told her heart to cooperate and allow her to return home and with this, her blood pressure fell in line and soon, the weeping followed. With a heart, broken but beating at a reasonable pace and her tears coming in short manageable spurts instead of gushing uncontrolled flurries, Madeleine was able to bear the absence and the empty, lonely silence at home and organise her cherished Harold a funeral. The whole time, she believed she could still feel him, like he hadn't really left her, like he was watching her, trying to work out a way to speak to her again. She sought desperately to see a sign from him, hoping every breeze, every play of the light, any change in temperature was him trying to communicate with her. So, when the strains of Nat King Cole singing 'Unforgettable' drifted out from a nearby house when she exited the taxi, she had taken to the church for her husband's funeral, Madeleine had believed wholeheartedly that it was Harold; after all, it was their song. With this cemented as fact in her mind, Madeleine was practically served up on a platter for Madame Marnie. She was waiting intently for the next sign from Harold when Madame Marnie tapped her on the shoulder and introduced herself.

The next day, Madeleine arrived early at Madame Marnie's, her jubilance at the prospect of holding one more real conversation with her Harold barely contained in the grinning expression on her face and the lightness of her bouncing step.

"Please, come in," Madame Marnie ushered her into her parlour. "I can feel Harold's spirit already; he is very eager to speak with you." She offered Madeleine the chair across from her own and as they both sat down, she began the act.

She started as she always did by taking a few deep breaths as she swept her arms at the same time in an arc out to the sides of her body and over her head.

"Hmm, yes, yes, he is here," Madame Marnie said, nodding slowly at Madeleine. "Just allow me a moment to open myself to him and we will proceed." Madame Marnie sat back in her chair with her face tilted towards the ceiling for a few moments before she proceeded.

"He wishes you not to be sad; he is watching over you; he needs you to be happy..." she trailed off, allowing a few moments more to pass, part of her act, feigning that it takes a lot of her energy to accommodate the communication.

Madeleine waited eagerly, trying not to be impatient, though as she bit her lower lip, she leant forward in her seat, her hands worrying its edge.

During all this time, Harold had indeed been watching and the actions of this conniving charlatan had awoken an anger in him, an anger that was charged not only by the manipulation of his wife's grief but by the ire of the entire spirit realm. And soon, Harold had little control over his actions, as he was assimilated into a vengeful army.

Just as Madame Marnie was readying herself to trot out some more of her usual diatribe, something happened; something changed in the room.

The temperature dropped rapidly and noticeably, with little puffs of fog suddenly issuing from both Madeleine's and Madame Marnie's mouths with their breath. The tapestries on the wall began to move, flapping as though being moved by a wind, but Marnie hadn't pulled on any of their attached fishing lines, nor as the candelabrum rocketed across the table, had she moved any of the corresponding magnets under the table. Madame Marnie's eyes widened, fear growing in her; she looked frantically around the room, trying to figure out what was happening, what had gone wrong with her apparatus. A movement brought her attention back to the table; the candelabrum rose a few inches off the table and smashed itself down into the crystal ball, sending shattered shards of glass flying past Madame Marnie, so close that they cut fine lines into her left cheek.

"What's going on, Marnie? Is that Harold?" Madeleine asked, a little scared at having sensed her fear.

*"**Madame** Marnie, I insist you must address me this way!" Madame Marnie almost yelled, her confusion and fear making her short with her customer, but still remembering to insist on the Madame, steadfast in the belief that affecting such*

eccentricities made her act more realistic.

"Of course, I'm so sorry, Madame Marnie, please, is Harold here?" Madeleine was still desperate to speak to her husband, though she was a little confused as to why he was hurling and breaking things and a tear slipped from her eye.

Madame Marnie was about to answer when, all of a sudden, she was rendered incapable; she felt as though she had been hit in the chest and stomach all at once; the air left her, and winded, she struggled to pull in breath. She felt something she had never felt before and all at once, she realised that the spirit realm was real and that not only was there a spirit present, but that it had entered her body.

"Madeleine, Madeleine, I am here, but please go home now; I will arrive there shortly and we will have a true discussion; you do not need this wicked fraud to speak with me. Go now and do not leave her any money." Madeleine rose in shock from her chair as Harold's voice issued from Madame Marnie's body. She hesitated for a moment until he continued, "Maddy Paddy, please, go now; I promise I will be there soon; how about I bring you a yellow rose and some peanut brittle?" Harold made Madame Marnie's face smile and her head nod.

"Oh, Harold, darling, I love you; yes, I'll go now; I'll see you at home." Madeleine's hesitation evaporated at the sound of Harold's pet name for her and the mention of the gift He had brought her on their first date.

"Thank you, Madame Marnie, thank you!" She gushed as she flew out the door, propelled by the weightlessness of her unbearable grief having suddenly halved.

Harold was soon going to meet his wife, but first, he had another task to complete, for he knew that he would never find true peace if he did not help bring the karma deserved to the *pitiful, loathsome being that had first been called Natalie, who then, twisted by sorrow and hardship believed was entitled to con and thieve by calling herself first Madame Zelda and then Madame Marnie.*

Madame Marnie never got the chance to protest, plead or present the facts that she believed exonerated herself. As soon as Madeleine was out of earshot, Harold planted himself further inside Madame Marnie and opening himself and her to the ire of the dishonoured spirit realm, he channelled that rage into two strong hands that gripped her neck tightly and then twisting, he broke her neck from the inside out. He and the rage left her broken body and Natalie Edgar, no longer Madame Zelda or Madame Marnie, fell to the floor, her neck twisted and her face contorted with not just her own fear at the end but the agony and the anguish of every grieving soul living and dead that she'd disgraced.

Harold Ferguson, now free from the anger that Natalie Edgar and her fake personas had generated, went home for one last visit and conversation with his wife. He handed her a yellow rose and a piece of peanut brittle and they spent the night reminiscing and saying their final goodbyes. When this was done, Harold Ferguson was finally able to rest in peace and Madeleine, though she never stopped loving him and missed him for the rest of her life, was able to finish grieving and move on.

That was the end of Natalie's story, and I went back outside to tell Kathy; she now sat surrounded by a litter of cigarette butts and had moved on to gnawing at her cuticles. But after a quick check back inside, I was able to assure her that the spirit who had been disturbing her family was now gone, her energy spent telling me her story. There was nothing to be scared of now. I could still sense the strange underlying panicky feeling and I assumed that it was the fear Kathy and her family had been experiencing, but now that its source was gone, I expected their fear to be gone also," Lily finished explaining the story to Hannah.

"But you weren't right about that part, were you?" Hannah asked her. "I saw something in the window, too," she added, explaining her question.

"I'm not sure yet, but yes, it seems that maybe I was wrong; I think that figure we saw in the window is Kathy or was Kathy," Lily admitted to Hannah.

Hannah nodded. "Are we going inside?" she asked, her intrigue outweighing her apprehension.

"Yes, I have to go in to find out if that figure was Kathy and hear her story," Lily explained, making sure to retrieve the clear quartz crystals she placed outside the car as they made their way up to the house.

As the two approached the house, with its windows like eyes, they felt it was watching them. Lily silently spoke in her mind to the figure she'd seen before, telling her, 'I'm ready now. I'm bringing a friend and we are here to listen to your story.'

"How are we going to get inside?" Hannah asked Lily as they mounted the front stairs.

"I don't think that's going to be a problem." Lily smiled as the front door, sitting in its colonial-style frame, swung out towards them. Hannah's mouth dropped open in amazement for a second but then shut promptly in almost shock as she realised that she could hear someone speaking to her, and it wasn't Lilly.

"Is, is that Kathy speaking to me?" Hannah asked, hopeful.

"Umm, I think so. It *is* Kathy and she is giving me a story; she has been waiting for someone to come along who could hear her. She's eager to be free from what is tying her here and pass on into peace," Lily answered with sadness in her voice; she could tell already that Kathy's story did not have a happy ending.

Lily and Hannah walked around the large, empty house together, coughing now and then from the dust and dodging the occasional cobweb. They could feel Kathy and the fear and sadness of her story in every room. They finally settled in a large upstairs bedroom to be told Kathy's story, the one that had been her and her husband George's in life, the room that had become her bedroom alone when she became the sole occupant of the house, her husband gone, taking Christopher with him. The room that she had eventually died in.

Lilly now realised, and Hannah became aware, that the different, edgy energy, separate from Natalie's, that she had felt twenty years prior was Kathy's fear – it had begun to transform into terror, an almost living neurosis, it had become its own entity born of Kathy's growing, impending insanity.

Although Lily had essentially cleansed Kathy's home of the spirit who had resided there, it no longer mattered; it wasn't enough, for the damage had been done to her mind. Despite Lily's assurances on the day she had visited, her husband's insistence and even a priest's blessing, Kathy continued to be afraid, and her fear soon grew into a consuming terror. She saw something that wasn't there everywhere. Everything was really something else, constantly convinced that Natalie, Madame Zelda or Madame Marnie was still there and despite knowing that all three had actually been one person, she had now become petrified of three separate beings, for although Natalie was gone, taking Madame's Zelda and Marnie with her, Kathy saw them every day, felt them everywhere, a continuous obsession that came to devour her completely. George had tried to get her help, but nothing did help; nothing could help. And when it was suggested to him that he look into having her institutionalised, he instead left with Christopher because he wasn't going to have his wife 'locked up in loony bin' and his son was so scared of her rantings by now that it seemed the best thing to do for everyone. Kathy noticed their absence and felt lonely and deserted, but her focus was more on the desperate need to preserve herself from the things that weren't there and yet were everywhere.

Kathy's days were spent in constant pain; her fear and anger, regret, sorrow, and loneliness manifested physically with an aching chest and head, churning stomach, lump in her throat, aching limbs, her whole body ached to her bones. She wandered lost around her empty house, dodging figures that were not there and existing in a perpetual state of highly strung, overwrought emotion, her fear matched only by her exhaustion.

The loneliness and sorrow she felt from having lost her family only exasperated her fears, and it was not long before the night came that Kathy took one too many sleeping pills with one too many vodkas and did not wake up. As she slipped away, her heavy slumber becoming death, she hallucinated Natalie in front of her, half of her dressed as Madame Zelda and the other half of her in the garb of Madame Marnie; she reached her hand out to Kathy, and Kathy, in death, suddenly no longer afraid, surrendered and took it.

After that, Kathy's spirit continued to wander the house, no longer scared but longing to be free, just waiting for someone to come and hear her story so that her energy could evaporate and she could finally rest and be free.

Neither Lily nor Hannah could be sure if Kathy meant to kill herself or not, and Kathy was unsure if she had taken all of those pills followed by all of those drinks with intent to die or just the hope that she might. But it was done now; she told both Lily and

Hannah and thanked them for listening to her story so that she could end her suffering.

Lily and Hannah left Kathy's house, now empty of all entities, the air around them abuzz in anticipation of the conversation regarding Hannah's emerging gift that was sure to follow on the car ride home.

Chapter Five: The Understudy: A Half Death

Lily had three last jobs booked before she was set to retire, and she had promised Hannah that she would take her on all three.

Before she could do this, though, she had to decide in which order to do the jobs. She opened the three emails requesting her services and looked them over, already knowing which one she would do last; there was no question there. It was which one to do first that she needed to consider. Her main consideration was Hannah; she had already exposed her to some fairly frightening stories in their excursions to locations from past jobs and although Hannah had fared quite well, Lily didn't want the first 'live' one to involve anything too malicious, especially since Hannah seemed to have a strengthening gift of seeing and speaking with spirits herself. Lily printed each request out and sat them in front of her on her desk; she read each one again and then cleared her mind as she laid a hand on each one in turn. The one that was asking her to do a reading on a home a young couple was about to move into seemed the most innocuous, and although Lily was able to sense the flashing lights of an ambulance, she sensed no lingering spirits with calamity in mind and so she chose this one for Hannah's first 'hands-on' experience of her work. A few emails back and forth saw Hannah organised to meet her the next day at the property in question and a quick phone call confirmed with her client, Melody, that she would meet Lily and Hannah at the location.

The Next Day:

The day of Hannah's first firsthand experience arrived quickly and as Lily introduced her as her protégé, she was surprised to find herself feeling nervous rather than delighted at the accolade.

In an effort to calm her nerves, Hannah asked permission to take some photos of the house and then readied herself to do so, as Melody confirmed that she didn't mind.

Melody hovered just inside the front door, slightly nervous, hoping she wasn't going to be told that her new home was haunted and feeling a little silly for even entertaining the idea. She had been afraid of ghosts and things like them for as long as she could remember. It was her mother's irrational fear, a fear bordering on paranoia that had rubbed off on her, a fear that she had spent most of her life burying, or at least she thought she had buried it.

When she'd told her mother that Justin and herself were moving into a house that'd been built in the late '70's, her mother had stirred those fears up in her again. So, when a friend had told her about Lily and her services, she had jumped at the idea, hoping it would allay her fears of moving into a new home with an unknown history.

"It's not silly to be scared of the unknown; lots of people are." Lily smiled at Melody, hoping it would calm her.

"Thanks," Melody said, smiling self-consciously as she looked down at her fingernails.

"Why don't you wait here with Hannah and I'll do a walkthrough of the house; I'll call you both when I have something. Okay?" Lily suggested. There was only a very quiet whisper coming from the house and a not quite spirit that was not quite there; Lily needed all of her concentration to hear the story and that would be near impossible with Hannah and Melody following her around.

"Okay." Melody agreed as Hannah nodded her approval, and the pair moved to sit on the window seat and chatted quietly.

Lily walked slowly around the house, pausing in each room. She started to hear the story a little louder in the main bedroom, but then she heard it coming stronger still from the bathroom doorway; she made her way there and called for Melody and Hannah to join her, where she relayed to them the following story:

Heather Logan was a thirty-seven-year-old art teacher when she collapsed half in half out of the bathroom after having gone to the toilet and washing her hands.

She never got up from that floor again. Three months later, though, she came home from the hospital in a wheelchair, disabled but lucky to be alive. She never taught in a classroom again, never crossed a road by herself, never left her home alone again and lived with a constant fear of dying, but she did walk again. And though half of her died that day, the half that pulled her through the horrific operation she needed to save her life from the biggest brain aneurysm rupture her neurosurgeon had ever seen, and the many complications that followed, complications that had killed all other cases on record, that's the half that survived and lived on – walking in Heather's body, like a driver, an understudy who had stepped in to take the lead role when the actor who'd been cast as the title character was too sick to perform. Heather 2.0, Heather Original told Lily, was better at the role than she'd ever been once she'd gotten used to her.

Although Heather Original had done some great things for herself (themselves), like picking herself up after being used, manipulated and treated abhorrently by someone she loved more than herself, and getting herself, eventually, out of a toxic and abusive relationship, and graduating with honours and on the Dean's merit list from a Master's degree in Education, Art and Literature; Heather 2.0 felt more real, she was more authentic to Heather's true self – she felt more deeply, and although that meant lower lows, it made the highs so much more joyful. Although her survival had demanded that half of herself be left behind to be able to survive, the other half of herself got to live a new life, with half of herself made up by a new person, a person who'd lived through incredible trauma, left with permanent impairments and parts of herself missing, a person who now had rearranged priorities, because it's amazing all the things you realise don't matter at all, when you'd come so close to death.

Although Heather's strong will to survive and the birth of Heather 2.0 played a major role in her survival, she knew that the credit couldn't go all to her; in fact, maybe the larger part of it needed to go to the love that gave her the will to live, the love that spoke to her, loud enough that she could hear it inside of her coma, strong enough that she could feel it pulling her out of a deep, deep sleep. Strong enough that even when her brain had swollen to a dangerous size and her organs were shutting down one by one, there was never one single second where succumbing to the tidal wave of the impossible challenge, not one single cell in her body was going to do anything but fight, and not just fight, but survive. Even before she had pulled herself from the incredible heaviness and overwhelming exhaustion that was the coma, she knew she was going to wake up and she was going home; she was going home to Gregory, her love.

Even before she was conscious again, she could feel him when he walked into her room; even through the weight of the coma, his presence changed everything. Her spirits were lifted, and her mood soared, her heart filled with love, divine happiness descending upon her when he was there. But of course, as with all such highs, there had to be the polar opposite low; long after visiting hours had ended, when someone would eventually come to kick him out, a deep despair would take over. Instead of yielding to it, Heather would instead spend the lonely hours concentrating on winning, on not dying. She'd focus also on the knowledge that he would come back; he was always coming back, he loved her, and he wasn't going anywhere. He believed in her, that she could do this, she would survive. When she was home, he'd tell her about the most optimistic thing he'd allowed himself to do, a gesture of deliberate hope; he'd carried her handbag with her glasses in it, knowing that she'd ask for them both as soon as she woke up, which she did.

And when she eventually was out of the coma, she would spend the lonely hours sleeping as much as she could and when she could sleep no longer, she would use her little energy to work as hard as she could in physical therapy so that she could tell Gregory something good when he arrived to visit her.

Eventually, she had worked so hard that it was time to go home.

But because it was Heather 2.0 that went home, nothing was ever quite the same again. Heather's circle had always tended to be small, but after the rupture, it became even smaller. Many of her friends didn't know how to treat her any more because although she was the same person, deep inside there, somewhere, she was vastly changed and didn't always act like the old Heather had; she wasn't always as driven, as confident, as independent, she wasn't as 'Heather'. They found her strange, stranger than she had been before. Heather Original had been very smart and even with brain damage, Heather 2.0 found herself to still be intelligent, sometimes more so than those around her; being smart had always made people resent her, so now that even a brain injury had not changed that, they resented her even more.

But she preferred to just live and do the things she enjoyed, leaving society and competition behind – living with a brain injury was a full-time job – even for Heather, who had had such a miraculous recovery. 'Recovery', she hated that word, it implied that she was better – she would never be better, there would never be a day when she woke up and would be the same as she was before she collapsed, because original, pre-rupture Heather was dead – she had to become post rupture Heather, Heather 2.0 to survive; there's a trauma that will live in her forever; the memory of being trapped in a coma where it felt like treading water, where it felt like living underwater, never quite reaching the surface no matter how hard she swam. Everything was heavy and she was so, so tired, but she knew she could not fall asleep. She fought the sleep that threatened to take her, but even without sleep, she had dreams anyway. Nightmare visions, horror movie pictures; a dead woman, skin glowing white and long hair as black as pitch, sitting beside her bed, beckoning her to go with her. Then voices would break through and she could hear how almost everyone thought she would die, but then she heard those begging her not to and she'd feel her love, Gregory and she pushed against the weight and the fatigue and ignored the tubes she could feel going up her nose and down her throat and she willed herself awake and back to life, in a body that now felt foreign, in a mind that seemed like a stranger, to an existence where the machine that controlled everything about her was damaged and **every single** action took so much more effort and energy (medical research says six times, but Heather puts it more at ten-twenty some days) for her than for everyone else. An existence in a world where she looked normal but felt too vulnerable for.

Heather had always been misunderstood but now it was worse because she didn't fit so many people's narrow-minded view of what disability looked like that they actually questioned her as to how she was disabled, they judged her and spoke behind her back, bitching amongst themselves that she should go back to work – while she spent days on end in bed, incapacitated by excruciating pain in her head that rendered her helpless – they didn't see these moments; they saw only what they wanted to see, like always – at school, they'd seen someone beating them in every test and better than them in most subjects – there they ignored the hard work she did and the choices she made to improve herself while they slacked off and chose differently, or poorly. They ignored or didn't remember the times when she had chosen differently and poorly, times that still came to haunt her at four o'clock in the morning when she couldn't sleep. Choices she'd made that she was still ashamed of to this day, even with everything that had happened to her. Times when she had faltered in her convictions and treated someone badly, or even dreadfully to fit in, or chosen the option she knew wasn't right and worse yet would hurt someone, just to please the more popular friend. Heather had apologised for most of this, but it still didn't sit right with her, even now. But most had continued to judge her for being 'goody two shoes' or 'straighty one – eighty', as they had sometimes teased.

Now they saw someone who could walk and talk and to them

was just like anyone else, who was saying they were disabled – ignoring what had been taken away from her; her mind being slowed down, her sharpness of wit being dulled, aphasia stealing her thoughts and words. Her eyes, though able to see, were blind on the left side of each; her confidence and faith in herself disappeared, her career stolen. Someone who had read Shakespeare for fun now struggled to get through Stephen King (though she always added when saying this, even to herself, that her remark was no slight to Stephen King; she loved his work, it just wasn't Shakespeare.), it taking her literally months to finish one of his books because of how tired reading made her and how often she had to stop to look up the meanings of words she'd known for most of her life that had now escaped her. She read and reread these familiar stories, though, because she felt safe in them; she needed the comfort, and for the same reason, she watched her old favourite shows and movies over and over.

They didn't understand that even though she was living a more authentic life, truer to herself, often she was living her life in four-hour increments, simply existing between the doses of pain medication. In these times, she was repeatedly almost swept away by waves of sadness that frequently accompanied the waves of pain. At times, she barely held on to herself and her more positive outlook, these moments with knuckles white and teeth clenched – the moment would pass to come again, but it would pass. And at other times still, fatigue would overcome her, seeping into every crevice of her being so that everything became dreamlike and she would wonder if she was in a dream; at these times, she'd wonder if she had died either on the floor half in, half out of the bathroom or later in the hospital, or maybe even on the way there, and that all of this, her new self and her new life was a dream, a dream within a dream.

They looked down on her because even with all she'd had to overcome and all the burden she now had to live with – they saw her as still better off than them and it ate them alive that she just kept living her own way, finding her own happiness and as much as possible not giving any time to all those who judged and misunderstood her. Her energy was too precious now and she knew that all that really mattered was her and Gregory and their happiness, so that was what they focused on.

Sometimes, it still all got to her though, the loss of self and the outside judgement, but she thought to herself: So much of her life before had been wasted in pursuit of useless things, things that wasted her time, her life – commuting to and from places by bus or train, places she usually did not want to go to – meaningless, stupid, boring jobs, or training for them, the lost hours in hated places, places that hurt to be in. And way too much time given to people who did not deserve it – fair weather friends, poorly chosen and unworthy partners, hangers-on. She had though, somehow always seemed to identify and appreciate the good people and the jobs and places that were less hateful and so not so useless and so not so much a waste of life. However, with all of this waste in a life that was so nearly taken away too early and then given back irrevocably changed – some for good, some for bad, she refused now to waste time on anything or anyone that did not inspire, uplift or in some way contribute positivity or deliver joy. And for that, she would not apologise and for those who didn't understand, didn't like it or wanted to judge her for it – be off with you, she said, for she has no time, no more of her precious energy, her precious life to waste on you!

"Lily, I have one more comment about this whole thing for you," Heather told Lily. "I always used to wonder what was wrong with me, why am I different, weird and 'apart' from almost *everybody else? Maybe now, with a brain injury, it's not actually that I'm a new person that I don't know, a new me in the same skin, the understudy of me, the character of 'girl with brain injury', it is, but it's more, it's actually that I'm more me now because now there's a real concrete cause, an answer for this 'off-ness' and I don't know if that's liberating or heartbreaking. But I can tell you that I savour every day, even when it's hard, even when I'm in pain, even when it's all getting me down. I love life now more than ever before,"* she finished, and Lily could see Heather smiling through tears that were both sad and happy but mainly eternally grateful to still be alive.

"Heather is still alive. She and Gregory moved away from here to somewhere peaceful, and they spend their time doing things they love. There's not any feeling of death in her story, only the parts of herself that were shed with her near-death experience; yes, in a sense, those parts did die, and I guess they do have a spirit and it's that that's telling me Heather's story, but it's not like a regular spirit, it's not really energy, it's more of an echo, or an imprint left behind," Lily told Melody and Hannah after relaying Heather's story.

"Do you think you'll sense it when she does die?" Hannah asked her, trying to understand the concept of someone losing half of themselves.

"Maybe, probably, if I concentrated on her, I could, but I think that when Heather does die, all of her, that her spirit will rest because her story has been told." Lily smiled as she explained to Hannah.

"There's not – there aren't any ghosts here?" Melody asked sheepishly.

"No, Melody, there's not. There's not anything here for you to fear. Although Heather experienced a great ordeal and had to mourn the loss of her old self and now lives with chronic pain and physical and cognitive dysfunctions, her story is ultimately a happy one and the energy that was left here that was able to give me her story is dissipating now, now that the story is told, the energy is spent. This is just an empty house where a girl survived a life-threatening incident and moved on to appreciate her life more, more loved and in love and more alive than ever before." Lily smiled at Melody.

"Thank you, thank you!" Melody gushed, letting out a long breath, so relieved and thrilled that her new home was ghost-free and charmed by the love story that was hiding in Heather's tale. Her relief was palpable, her body lost the rigidity she had been holding herself with and her face softened as her fear left her.

Lily instructed Hannah to take some photos of the doorway where Heather had collapsed and then they moved outside so she could take a couple more of the house from outside.

"I'll send you a copy of any photos I want to use in my book for your approval before publishing," Lily assured Melody as they readied to leave.

"Thank you." Melody nodded, smiling.

"I'd love to read it when it comes out, but I can't promise anything because ghosts freak me out!" she admitted with a grin.

"Most of the ghosts move on after they've told Lily their stories, so maybe you wouldn't be so scared by Lily's book," Hannah suggested.

"Hmm, maybe. Maybe I'll give it a try," Melody yielded, more open to the possibility now.

"OK, I'll have Hannah email you when it comes out," Lily replied and moved towards her car with Hannah.

"Thank you again, Lily; I feel so much better about moving in here now," Melody admitted.

The three exchanged goodbyes. Melody left excited to tell her mother that her new home was most certainly not haunted and to tell Justin about the bittersweet history of their new home.

Hannah went back to her uni res room with a whole new angle to add to her PhD dissertation.

Lily went home to prepare for her last two jobs so that she could retire and return home to rest.

Chapter Six: The Other Katie: A Ghost Story

One of Lily's last jobs was one of her most mysterious. She had received an email from a woman in England whose daughter had been missing for many years, though she had received one postcard from her, it was a picture of a gypsy caravan, and on the back, it said:

Dear Mother,

I am gone now, though I am no longer sure which of the two of us I am.

From,

~~Katie~~ The Other Katie.

The postcard had been mailed from Gleaman village in Australia. The village was actually a small town just outside of Bellton. The woman had been unsure of when or even if Katie had actually travelled to Australia, but she had told Lily that her daughter had always been strange and had spent her life since the age of sixteen trying to outrun an imaginary curse. She further described that many times throughout her life, Katie had felt someone was watching her through reflective surfaces: puddles, windows, mirrors, anything that could cast back her image. Her parents had always been dismissive of Katie and her notions of being watched, rejecting her feelings and the people she said were watching her as being imaginary; as even before she'd started imagining people watching her and blathering about a family curse, she had been obsessed with scary things; it had taken over her whole life.

In email communications back and forth with Katie's family, Lily had ascertained that by 'scary things' they had meant all things macabre and occult – Katie had been a lover of scary stories, ghosts and horror movies, or any material that she could get her hands on that included ghosts, witches, curses or hauntings. Her fixation on these had been to the exclusion of almost all else. Her compulsive appetite for the dark and supernatural left her an outcast, though she never complained of being lonely; rather, she seemed to embrace it, as it was more in line with the themes of her many beloved stories.

Lily also learned that Katie had planned to travel to Scotland to see the eerie and haunted places that were depicted in many of the movies and books she devoured. In her last communication with her family before seeming to vanish without a trace, she had indicated that was where she was going. No one had seen or heard from her since, except for the strange postcard. Police investigations had turned up nothing and no one from her neighbourhood or anywhere else could vouch for having seen her.

With no address to visit, Lily requested the postcard be sent to her. By the time it arrived, she was doubtful of finding any definitive answers for Katie's family, but she was determined to find out what she could.

Postcard in hand, Lily led Hannah to Gleaman village. The place was a sleepy town that time had left behind; it still had only one shop, a general store that also served as news agency and post office, there was a pub and a tiny police station. The rest of the village was made up with farms and fields; many people who lived there needed to drive to get to their letterboxes, let alone their next-door neighbours.

Lily and Hannah drove around Gleaman quietly for half an hour before Lily suddenly pulled her car to the side of the road and instructed Hannah that they needed to walk from there.

Lily had explained to Hannah in an early morning conversation over coffee before setting off on their journey the reason she didn't have an exact location for them to visit, but had added that she was confident she'd sense a more precise position for them to attend once they were there.

"I can feel something up there," she told Hannah, gesturing further up the road, past a glen of trees.

"Let's go!" Hannah urged, excited to be part of figuring out the mystery.

The pair hiked up the gentle slope of a hill, beginning to puff a little as it became much steeper. Neither spoke, not from exertion but from the understanding that Lily needed quiet to follow the whispering directions she was getting from the ether.

Soon, they reached the trees Lily had indicated, and as they rounded the edge of them, Lily stopped abruptly as a gypsy caravan, the same as the one on the postcard, seemed to appear out of nowhere.

"This is it; this is where Katie is, or where her story is at least," Lily clarified. The pair took a moment to absorb the sight; the caravan was small and made up of light pink timber panels, its roof curved and its windows made from brightly coloured stained glass, one a rose, another St Jude, Patron saint of lost souls and the last, Saint Sarah, patron Saint of Misfits.

Lily instructed Hannah to take some photos of the caravan, especially the windows, and whilst Hannah did so, Lily walked towards the caravan door. It didn't open up for her, like the doors of the asylum had, but it wasn't locked.

"I'm going inside; I'm not sure if we're both going to fit at the same time," Lily told Hannah as she carefully mounted the mouldering makeshift stairs and ducked in through the front door.

Standing inside the tiny caravan, Lily could feel the many different places that Katie had towed it to, the many divergent towns and cities, the backwoods and the boondocks, all the places she'd lived at but couldn't stay put in. And all the time, she was moving from one place to the next, every road she took, every shortcut, every highway, every dirt road track, always outrunning the family curse, outrunning the watcher from the reflective surfaces.

Lily took in the interior; it was beautiful, its walls clad with a rich mahogany timber. A compact table and bench that could be folded out into a mini lounge upholstered in a rose-patterned fabric. And the miniature kitchen hid inside a double-door cupboard next to even tinier bathroom, hiding in a corner with a wavy glass door. An archway with a curtain gave way to a bed that lifted up to reveal a storage space for clothes and shelves built into the wall. Lily scoured all the shelves, cupboards and secret hiding storage places, there was nothing. But when she turned to tell Hannah she could come inside, she noticed the pieces of a broken mirror on the floor. All at once, Katie's story came to her, flooding her senses, almost overwhelming in its urgency to be heard.

"This one's a ghost story," Lily told Hannah as she stepped inside the caravan.

"Aren't they all?" Hannah asked, a little confused.

"Not really, the others are people stories – just because they are being told to me posthumously by a spirit doesn't make them ghost stories." She smiled. "But this one is," she clarified before relaying Katie's story to her.

Lily cleared her throat and repeated the story she'd just been told to Hannah:

*

"It was a dark and stormy night when Katie Brown arrived at Adlestone Manor. Black clouds swirled in an even blacker sky, spitting sharpened shards of water into her back as she struggled with her suitcase from her car to the front door. The manor loomed imposingly before her, two storeys of peeling, sagging timber with gaping window eyes that watched her arrival. Katie let herself in and fumbled around until she found a light switch, pulling from her pocket the photograph that had been given to her along with the keys to the foreboding house. Wandering into the front room, Katie sank into an armchair shrouded in a dust cover as her eyes traced the features of the face in the picture, the same features that she saw in the mirror every day, but the face in the picture was not her own. Three weeks earlier, Katie had been contacted by a lawyer who told her she had inherited Adlestone Manor from a cousin she had never heard of who also shared her name. Katie had disbelieved the entire story and a little investigation into her family tree couldn't find any trace of the woman. The lawyer, persistent, had contacted her again, this time with all the relevant paperwork for the house and a photograph of her cousin. The woman in the picture looked exactly like Katie. Katie shook her head and crammed the photo back into her pocket; it didn't make any sense; none of it did.

Katie climbed the stairs to look for a bedroom; she was suddenly very, very tired and could think of nothing else but sleep. The first room she looked in seemed familiar, and stripping back the dust covers revealed it to be the room in which the photograph had been taken. Too exhausted to care or even notice that the sheets were surprisingly clean, she climbed into the bed, inviting with blankets and pillows, her mind slipping into the shadowy, foggy place between waking and sleeping; she smiled as she wondered if the pillow knew the difference between her and her cousin.

It didn't take long for Katie to begin dreaming, but her dream didn't take her too far away; she was dreaming of the room she was sleeping in. It was dark but there was a light shining on a mirror that hung on the wall. The mirror began to fog as she moved towards it. "Dear Diary," A voice whispered as Katie woke up.

Katie awoke with the whisper still in her ear, it drove her out of the bed. Suddenly, she felt very vulnerable in this big, old, empty house and perhaps even a little bit stupid for coming to this place alone. She left the bedroom in search of a bathroom, finding it across the hall. She ran warm water into the basin, thankful when the steam clouded her reflection; she was sick of it reminding her of the woman in the picture. She washed her face, massaging the taught skin at her temples. Katie gasped as she looked up; in the fog on the mirror was written 'Dear Diary'. The reflection behind the steam smiled back at her, but Katie wasn't smiling. She screamed and ran from the bathroom back to the bedroom. A shaft of light filtered through the room's heavy curtains, falling on the mirror. Katie moved towards it. Its reflection grew foggy and words began to form on its surface. Katie lunged at it, knocking it from its position on the wall. The mirror shattered as it fell to the floor. Where the mirror had hung was a rough hole in the wall. Katie reached in as compulsion overtook any reluctance, pulling out a small leather-bound book. She knew what it was before she had even turned to the first page;

Dear Diary,
It read.
The other is coming for me now; I can feel it getting closer. It has followed me all my life, waiting for this moment. When I was young, my grandmother told me the story of the family curse– hundreds of years ago, a woman on the Adlestone side of the family had an affair with a gypsy travelling through the town; she fell pregnant with twins to this man. His wife found out and placed a curse on the woman, that one of her twins would be trapped in the mirror world, never to escape except by luring another to take her place. This curse was never to end, and it has not ended. I have seen her in the mirror mocking me; the other, she follows me everywhere and she calls to me, and I cannot resist her for much longer now.

Katie shut the diary and looked down at the shards of mirror encircling her. In each one, she could see her face, but it was not her face; it was the other Katie's face and the other Katie was calling her, calling her, and Katie knew she could not resist much longer."

"And then what?" Hannah asked, looking at Lily with wide eyes, eager for the next part of the story.

"That's it," Lily told her.

"What do you mean, that's it? That can't be the end, what happened?" Hannah asked insistently.

"That's it, that's all Katie told me. She didn't even really tell me she was not here; she just left her story behind for someone like me to come along and hear it. Sometimes, the spirits don't want to give up their whole story. And the walls of this abode certainly don't know," Lily gave by way of explanation.

"So, is she dead? Where is she?" Hannah entreated.

"I don't know for sure. I think she's dead because the story has come to me from 'the other' realm. The best explanation I can give is that the story itself has become a spirit; it's like Katie became her own ghost story and she just doesn't exist any more – except inside the story. And that's what she wanted, to be the thing she loved most – a ghost story," Lily clarified.

"Isn't that sad? That she wanted to be a ghost story?" Hannah asked with a hint of melancholy in her voice.

"No," Lily replied. "It's what she wanted – sometimes people are in a ghost story, and they don't even know it. It's not always a dark and stormy night," Lily said as they walked back to her car in the bright sun.

Hannah asked a few more questions, desperate for closure, and Lily was eventually able to convince her that there was no more to be told, telling her, "That's all she wrote."

The two headed back to Bellton, Hannah to email Lily the photos and recordings from the day and Lily to email her findings to Katie's parents.

Lily's email explained that she believed their daughter to be dead because her story was delivered to her from the spirit world. She included a copy of the same story she's been told in Katie's caravan, explaining that she was very sorry that she couldn't sense anything else and so could offer them no further explanation. She didn't tell the family that she did sense that there was a curse, a curse that could possibly have been broken to set both Katie's free, and she also left out that wherever Katie was, it didn't seem restful; she could sense a struggle like one of them was still trying to get out. Lily had not told Hannah that either; she had sensed that there was a danger and she knew from the teachings of her family's book that in such situations where the spirits would not or could not speak, there was little to be done by mortals. Lily knew the best she could do for Katie was to tell her story, so that's what she did. She also left the shards of broken mirrors behind in case someone with the powers or knowledge to break the curse ever came along; they might need them. Lily was fairly certain that the caravan would appear only to those who could hear Katie's story and certainly to those who could break a centuries-old curse.

Chapter Seven: Sarah's Story

Pulling up to the address sent to her the day before, Hannah looked for Lily, who was usually waiting outside; not finding her there, she made her way into the apartment block and walked towards the door number Lily had given her. As she arrived outside number 9, she was curious to still find no trace of Lily but finding the door ajar, she entered to find the woman in question gazing at a wall.

"Am I late?" Hannah questioned when she found Lily already inside instead of waiting for her out front.

"No, not at all, right on time." Lily smiled; she seemed happier today, lighter than usual, Hannah noticed.

"Oh good, I wouldn't want to be late for our last day." Hannah smiled eagerly.

"I think it's appropriate for this story for you to take a photo of all of the rooms, and particularly, this window, this wall, and this wall," Lily explained, gesturing and moving to another room to point out the second wall she mentioned.

"Okay.," Hannah agreed and moved to do as she'd been instructed, thinking to herself that this job seemed different; it felt to her as though Lily maybe already knew this story.

"Where did this job come from?" Hannah asked when she'd finished with Lily's instructions.

"A neighbour of Sarah's contacted me; she'd lived in this building for some years and was interested in her story," Lily said. Hannah sensed more in her words than what she was really saying, but knowing Lily as she did now, she knew that by the end of the day, her questions would most likely be all answered.

"Now, I won't be able to stay around very long after I've finished telling you Sarah's story, so we're going to have to make sure that you have everything you need," Lily told Hannah with a smile Hannah remembered from the first day they'd met, one that she'd used when telling her she was older than she looked.

"Do you have an appointment to get to?" Hannah asked.

"Something like that," Lily told her, again the words laden with more than what they or the tone was revealing.

"Okay then, let's get started," Hannah said, not only so that Lily could get her job done and get off to wherever she needed to go, but to have her own curiosity allayed, both of Sarah's story and of the mysteriousness Lily was giving off that day.

"Yes, let's; I can hear Sarah already," Lily told her and waited for her to start recording on her phone before she began.

"She couldn't remember the exact moment or even the reason why the final catalyst came to be. Little by little, for maybe twelve years or so now, the panic and anxiety, the dread and the overwhelming sense of negativity had been growing every time she left her apartment; she'd been swallowing it all of those years, and each time, it had become a harder, more difficult, bigger piece of crazy to get down her throat, choking her. It hadn't mattered if it had been to go to work or to go shopping, to meet friends or to get some exercise; the result had still been the same, though growing in immensity and significance each time; at first, it had been a slight feeling of unease, maybe she would have called it nervousness or just feeling 'a bit off', slowly over a few months to a year, the slight agitation had become a more obvious disease, a sense of anxiety that manifested itself physically with stomach cramps and nausea, tremors, rashes,

and of course the crying. All of this Sarah had been able to hide at first – even the crying she'd been able hold off until making it to a public bathroom stall most of the time. Until slowly her control over that slipped away, the crying would come suddenly, violently, wracking her body and shooting out of her messy, snotty and brutal.

Through all of this, anything and everything outside of her home became at first difficult and then impossible. And then, one day, it was finally all too impossible to leave her home, let alone contemplate the thought of locking the door behind her and walking out into the world.

She didn't know where the sadness and the fear came from; she just knew it was there and it got worse and worse when she went outside until all she knew was that the attack of depression and panic that crippled her didn't occur when she was safely inside her home.

The day that Sarah referred to as 'the catalyst', the day that led to her no longer being able to leave her home, she hadn't been doing so well at swallowing her pain for weeks, and the day she'd just finished off, choking down the fear turned to pain constantly was still sitting on her uncomfortably. So, after reading a few chapters of a book, she started to flick through channels distractedly until the image filling the screen before sent her running from the room, too late, it seemed. The scene that had scared her so was a shot of an ugly, dirty man, like a tramp, dressed as a scarecrow, holding the arm of a strange small woman wearing the clothes and makeup of a doll. Those faces so terrifying; Sarah didn't know why or even how, but the image of those two strange people, the scarecrow and the doll, broke something inside of her, and whatever it was that had been broken was never going to be fixed again. The fear invoked by those faces, strong and irrational, loomed so large and uncontrollable that she could never control her fear enough to go outside ever again.

The next morning, Sarah did not even consider leaving her apartment, not seriously anyway and nor did she ever again. Not physically, anyway.

Yesterday (Sarah's last day outside):

The last time she was able to leave her apartment, in her mind at least, it had seemed somewhat of a big day, packed with things to do, and even now, many years later, as Sarah told her story to Lily and even with her having had many uninterrupted years to think about it, she still wasn't sure if maybe deep down somewhere inside of herself, she knew that it was going to be the last time, that a catalyst was coming.

*Sarah's hand shot out blindly, groping for her phone to silence the alarm. Shifting under the heavy mound of blankets, sleep not only still crusted her hazel eyes but held the left one glued shut; she rubbed at it as she lifted her body up to sit on the side of her bed. She let herself sit there for a few moments, willing herself to be more awake as she trudged to the bathroom. It finally worked and she found herself washing her face and brushing her auburn hair. Whilst doing so, she became aware of a dread, **the** dread as she knew it, slowly but then surely and firmly creeping first over her and then into her. A soft sort of sick feeling, not hard and heavy like the full body pervasion of the chills and nausea of the flu, but the slight distraction of an almost headache and a slight sadness, a dull, not quite there pain in the stomach and a slight nervousness that crawled over her skin, she pushed the sensation down inside of her and focused on the more* *pressing feeling of duty – the duty of being productive, of dropping off the signed paperwork at her job that would then allow her to work remotely, doing her proofreading and editing from home, or from wherever she desired as long as she could use a laptop.*

Part of her saw this as a release from the growing more prevalent discomfort of leaving for work; part of her told herself it was a cop-out and she was being weak. What she didn't know yet was that by tomorrow, the choice would be made for her anyway by means she would never fully understand or be able to control.

The duty of also seeing her friends, the friends that she'd cancelled on one shy of too many times. The duty of, she told herself as she tried to select an outfit, of being normal and not being so pathetic and weak over normal things that everyone had to do, things like leaving the house, going to work and leaving the house and meeting with friends. Shut up, she told herself, selecting the slightly old, back in fashion again Indigo-coloured bootcut jeans. She glanced at her watch, observing she was running a few minutes late as she rummaged through a pile of black t-shirts in a drawer, looking for the one with a small pocket over the left breast that she favoured.

She laced up white Converse high-top shoes and put her phone and a bottle of water in her large black handbag. Then she opened the front door to leave without eating breakfast, shoving the paperwork for her work in the bag, too. She was running late now and the not-quite-there pains and sick feeling had well established themselves into a lump in her throat and a lead in her stomach that would be allowing no food to pass through or stay down. Shutting the front door behind her took an army of strength and as Sarah looked down the corridor from her apartment towards the elevator, the floor seemed to rise up and the walls warp in and out; she put her head down, jaw rigid with arms tight at her side, fists clenched and forced her feet one after the other to move along. The concentration that it took to control her breathing and keep reign on the growling, growing dread that was turning into terror consumed her until she found herself, not knowing exactly how she'd arrived there, at the door of the elevator that would take her to her office. A firm band of steel tightened around her head as it pulsed against the constraint; bile kept rising from her stomach to her throat lump, where she was able to choke it down again. Her skin alternated between clammy and slick to tight and goose-pimpled, her breathing jagged and shaky with the manual in and out. Her heart beat so that she doubted the offbeat was detectable between beats at all. Sarah heard the doors to the street open behind her, pulling her from her hellish reverie and for an instant, she almost turned and ran. Instead, she pressed the button for the elevator and made her way upstairs to the twelfth floor to be the normal person that she told herself she needed to be. By the time the elevator had arrived at her destination, she'd swallowed her tears and the fear and had a veneer of composure in place again. She pushed the door to Preston Publishing open and walked in smoothly, calmly, with a well-hidden sense of self-consciousness.

"Hi, Tammy!" she called only a little too loudly to the receptionist.

"Sarah!" Tammy responded happily, standing up to greet her. "Olivia's in a meeting with a new client at the moment, but she said you'd be coming in to drop off your paperwork."

"Yeah, that's what I'm here for." Sarah smiled and took the large envelope of papers from her bag. "All signed and ready." She handed them to Tammy.

"You're so lucky! I wish I could work from home!" Tammy bubbled.

"Yeah, I guess I am," Sarah agreed, ignoring the sense of misplaced guilt over the arrangement that benefited everyone involved – but still, the strange guilt sat there.

"Oh hey, we've organised a little going away party for you. It was supposed to be this afternoon, but now Olivia has meetings all day, so I guess we'll have to do it tomorrow. Come in tomorrow at one, okay?" Tammy looked at Sarah expectantly.

Sarah crumpled inside but eked out. "Um, yeah, okay, great, see you then." Knowing there was little chance of her attending.

"I have to go now, Tammy; thanks." She waved and left before Tammy could add a 'see you tomorrow.'

The journey out of the office building and onto the street was much easier and much more welcome. Her phone vibrated in her bag with a message telling her she was late, and Sarah steeled herself for the next part of her 'being normal', meeting with her friends for brunch, which was now closer to lunch, she realised as somehow time had closed in on twelve thirty p.m.

Meeting up with her friends was a duty; it was a performance – the performance of 'I'm normal like you'. Sarah had known these friends for years, but somewhere, years ago, she'd changed and become so different from herself and from them, but somehow, they hadn't seemed to notice; either that or they hadn't really cared.

Sarah quickened her pace, weaving in and out of the people on the footpaths, walking as hastily as she could to get to her destination. She was slightly breathless as she arrived at 'The No 9 Cafe', where her friends were waiting. She stopped to catch her breath and took a few sips of water from the bottle in her bag and further ignored her not being okay-ness. Ready, she moved to enter the café and the automatic doors stayed shut, as though she wasn't there, as though she didn't exist, being short it wasn't the first time it had happened to her, she rolled her eyes waved her right arm above her head. It worked and the doors slid open. She spied Jackie and Ella towards the back of the café and pretended not to notice them abruptly stop speaking as she neared.

"I'm so sorry I'm late," Sarah said to both of them, only half true.

They assured her it was okay. "We're used to your lateness, Sarah." Ella smiled. "We'd be worried if you were on time!" The usual banter met with a soft laugh from the three of them.

"So anyway, how have you been?" Jackie asked.

"Oh, you know, just normal me, working and cancelling plans." Sarah gave what she hoped looked like a sincere and apologetic smile. "You two?"

"Good. It's just normal for me too, busy with the kids," Jackie replied.

"Same," Ella chimed in, nodding.

Sarah tried not to entertain the thought, trying to inject itself into her head that her friends were thinking she had it easy not having kids and judging her for it. She tried to tell herself firmly that it was just her anxiety talking; it wasn't true; no one was judging her. She could feel her heart rate quickening slightly.

"Have you guys ordered yet?" she asked, distracting herself.

"No, not yet, I'll grab us some menus," Ella offered

Sarah let herself be talked into a chocolate croissant that she mostly only toyed with and ordered a black tea instead of the coffees her friends were ordering.

"So, how is your work going?" Ella asked after their orders had been taken.

"Good." Sarah nodded. "I get to read so many different things. Sometimes it's boring though, last month I was proofreading a medical textbook and I didn't understand any of it! At least I don't need to understand what it's about; just find any spelling mistakes or punctuation errors. Sometimes it's fun, though, like the kid's book series I'm doing at the moment; they're really cute stories, much easier going than the anatomy stuff," Sarah told them.

What followed was a somewhat forced, slightly painful back and forth of further polite questions and answers about each other's jobs, the obligatory questions about Jackie and Ella's kids and partners and all of them trying to ignore that Sarah had none of the latter two.

By the time their croissants, doughnuts and sandwiches were remnants and their cups empty, Sarah felt enough time had passed for it to not be rude for her to try and extract herself. Luckily, more time had passed than she'd realised, and Jackie and Ella had begun making the 'need to pick up the kids from school' noises and Sarah was off the hook.

"We'll have to do this more often Sarah, if you can fit us into your busy schedule," Ella said with only slight sarcasm as she stood up to leave.

"Yes!" Jackie agreed eagerly.

"Yeah, we should; I'm so slack, I know; I just keep getting so busy with work. I'm really sorry, guys," Sarah said, putting an arm around them both. There was a quick three-person embrace before they made their final goodbyes and went their separate ways.

Sarah wasn't sure whether she wanted to wander around some shops or just go home; she started walking towards a shoe shop up the road when a low rumble of thunder in the distance changed her mind. Instead, she turned and started towards the taxi rank, heading for home for what turned out to be the last time. Sometimes, for the first month or so, she would wonder if she had known what was about to happen, what was about to change in her irreversibly forever – would she have stayed out? She was never really able to come to an answer that she knew to be true because when she looked back on that day, it was from a changed mind, almost a different person.

Hours later, with a storm starting to fizzle out, Sarah had washed the day from her and yet there was still some remnant of the dread that she couldn't quite be free of, like there was something hanging over her that she could never fully free herself from. Instead of focusing on it, trying to lay a finger on the exact source of her disquiet, she dressed herself in her favourite at-home ensemble of old black yoga pants and an even older baggy T-shirt, whatever band or frontman who'd once been emblazoned on it, long since faded and peeled away. She needed not distraction, but to fill her mind with something else, she sought out her copy of 'Crime and Punishment', a text so heavy and a story so involved that for hours after sitting herself down on the lounge with it, no stray thoughts, or thoughts of her own troubled her at all. Some many hours later, Sarah finished up the chapter she was on and decided she needed a break from Rodion Raskolnikov, as she was starting to feel as though she was descending into madness with him.

Instead, she turned on the television and started flicking through the channels. She reeled backwards in horror and the remote fell from her hand, forcing her to take in the image that filled the screen for longer than she wanted to.

"She wants to tell me about this incident again," Lily told Hannah. "She wants to make sure that it's understood how important this moment was, that this was the thing that finally broke her."

"*An ugly, dirty man, like a tramp dressed as a scarecrow, held the arm of a strange small woman who was dressed like and wore the makeup of a doll. Sarah's breath caught in her throat, a cold sweat broke out over her body; she was shaking so that it took her three attempts to retrieve the controller and change the channel to something else, something, anything other than the images invoking pure terror within her now. She shut her eyes, rubbing her hands against them and ran from the room, even though the image was gone. Those faces, those people, something so unnerving, so terrifying, she didn't know why or even how, but those two strange people, the scarecrow and the doll, had just broken Sarah Sienna Spare irrevocably, something inside of her had shattered and it was never going to be fixed again.*

The next morning, after quickly composing and sending a text message making her excuses for not attending the party at her office, she had thoughts of testing herself with leaving the apartment, not to go anywhere, just a small test, just to go outside of the door and come back in, and being as that she had herself screaming at her that she was weak, she performed the test. She got through the door, one step, two steps, and there it was, all of the anxiety and sadness she'd ever felt previously, combined with a newly ferocious terror that had been born when the scarecrow and doll people had broken her the night before, it broke over her, not as a wave but a tsunami. She turned and shot back through the door, slamming it shut and locking out the world and with it and a good portion of her terror. The longer she kept it shut and failed to entertain the idea of going outside, the better she felt: safer, less fear, less anxiety and less sadness.

After a time, maybe a few weeks, she stopped thinking about it and new routines and a new life evolved. The safety of her apartment soothed her so that the fortnightly opening of the door to drag in boxes of groceries elicited only a very slight feeling of panic and a headache that now only lasted a few hours instead of the initial panic attack, hyperventilation, vomiting and four-day migraine.

As this new sense of safety and angst-free existence grew, Sarah noticed that she'd stopped feeling guilty and berating herself for being weak and for not being normal. Instead, she just existed. Her existence in this safe haven stretched over many, many years, so many that Sarah lost count, so many days inside. In all of those days, they began to run into one another, but still, some stood out, and some stood out much more than others. Those days, though, came much later in Sarah's self-imposed exile; they came when she stopped existing purely inside of her own head, the walls of her apartment and the pages of the books lining her walls.

The first days of Sarah's new inside life, free from fear, she became intimate with every inch of her home. She roamed slowly through each room, stopping and taking in the size, the colours, the shape and the way she felt in each one. In her large lounge room, she ran her fingers over the wall of exposed brick and found its bumpy texture somehow comforting. Comfort, too, came from the deep blue of the worn carpet that gave way to ageing floorboards for the dining area that turned into tile for the tiny kitchen to begin. She stood at the edge of the kitchen, back against its bench, where she could take in the whole living and dining area of her home; she scanned from large street-facing window, currently with blinds tightly shut, up to the ceiling. She'd never quite realised how high her ceilings were; it was those high ceilings, she often felt, years later in contemplation of *her strange inside life, that had kept her from feeling trapped. As she turned to allow herself to see through the doorway of the spare bedroom, the room she called a study, her eyes caught the walls lined with bookshelves overflowing with books. Sarah's feet padded softly yet quickly, feeling such a sudden pull towards her books and the lives inside them. For a time, maybe months, if pressed to measure, she would have guessed maybe a year, maybe more – those books became her life; she read and re-read every single one of them. Partway through this mammoth expedition, Sarah recalled the words of her much loved high school English teacher who'd spoken of how some people, at some stages of their lives, may have nothing more to sustain them than great art and literature. Sarah had thought she'd understood this earlier in her adult life when she'd floundered with direction, lived with depression and spent most of her waking moments feeling less than, but now, now when the thing inside her holding all the loose threads together had finally broken, and the only way she could find to survive was to live inside forever, she thought she understood and appreciated the notion on a much deeper, more poignant level. She lived whole lives this way, visiting all of the places she'd once wished to go to, experiencing the people and cultures she'd always wanted to encounter, all of the sights she'd longed to see – she experienced them all; the people, the places, all of the experiences she'd ever hoped for, she lived them all within in the worlds of the books she read, and that was enough for her, which was lucky because now it was the only way she was ever going to realise that dream.*

Sarah began her journey through literature clad again in her favourite at-home ensemble of the old black yoga pants and the even older T-shirt who, over years of wash and wear, had become baggy and thin, the band or front man once emblazoning it long since faded and peeled away. The shirt held a far-off memory of a version of herself she felt long gone: a music festival attended with a nonchalance that had long since left her. Now her attendance was to a festival of words and imagination, she reopened, for the first time in many years, her copy of Orwell's 'Keep the Aspidistra Flying' The book had been old when she'd purchased it, the stamp of the second-hand bookshop already fading inside its cover. For an entire day, Sarah lived not inside her mind or even her own four walls. Instead, she visited another place; she dwelled inside George Orwell's much too apt rendering of poverty and scraping by, his painfully authentic creation of Gordon Comstock's neuroticism and tangibly agonising rationing of cigarettes. So perfect a portrayal of the pangs of poverty, hunger and disdain for the money machine he had created that they had hit so close to home the first time Sarah had read it that she had been disturbedly unsettled by its familiarity. Now, though, years later, with a distance between her and such a life, she was able to retake the journey of Gordon Comstock without it stirring in her a craving for a cigarette or dredging up the painful longing lacking of poverty. She wasn't sure if it was her own self-imposed hermetism, which did seem to come with a rejection of capitalism, that helped her to stay more of a distant spectator than an unwilling participant on her second and subsequent readings, but whatever it was she now welcomed the too sharp reality in those pages.

Next, ignoring the ringing phone, Sarah moved to her familiar 'Steppenwolf', which, even after many years, seemed to still speak to her soul, some of it so true to her that she could have been whispering into Herman Hesse's ear when he'd been writing it. Though the tale did threaten to awaken loneliness in Sarah, with its despondency and darkness, instead she embraced *it, finding in Henry Haller somewhat of a kindred spirit she could identify with. She returned the book to its shelf at its end with a quiet satisfaction, feeling that her soul had been fed.*

Such a long time, a timeless time for Sarah, went by like this: pessimism turning to hope with '1984', and tragedy after tragedy, 'Hamlet', 'The Bell Jar', 'Wuthering Heights', 'The Great Gatsby', 'Flowers for Algernon,'. Even 'Crime and Punishment', that she opened once again with a knowledge that it was an arduous journey to take; on her first trek with Dostoevsky, she'd felt her own sanity waning, and this time, once again, she felt as though she's started to decline alongside Rodion Raskolnikov, as though he was taking her with him into his final descent into insanity. Sarah closed the book, putting it back in its spot on the well-packed shelves. She felt a little tired, but as she left the room packed with books, with friends, she felt satisfied; she'd been fed; all the stories she'd devoured feeding her soul, A friend found in Winston, in Hamlet, in Esther, in Heathcliff, in Jay, in Charlie, in Rodion. She was companioned by them all, all feeding her soul, her secret self, who inside her new, solitary, insular, safe at-home world – no longer needed to be secret at all. She was filled up, nurtured, and sustained by these tomes, removing the need for Sarah for any input from the outside world. So, she ignored the phone when it rang, failed to return messages from her friends, and eventually, the interruptions from her former life stopped trying to reach her at all.

But she knew that that time was at an end; she now needed to seek sustenance from elsewhere. Sarah stood in the doorway of the study for a moment, casting her eyes over the books that had consumed her and been consumed by her; she said silent thanks to them all and then moved to the large street-facing window that sat between her lounge room and dining area. She pulled open the heavy blue curtains that matched the carpet and raised the blind; it had been weeks, months? Some time, she resigned since she'd let the natural light in, since she'd allowed a portal to the tangible outside. She stood for a moment and gazed out at the world, the world outside her head and outside her home. She blinked in rapid succession for the first minute, her hazel eyes adjusting to the new brightness. She moved closer to the window as her eyes grew accustomed to the light; for a moment, she looked down at her hands resting on the window sill; they were pale, a little thinner and a little more lined and older looking than she remembered. Soon, some movement below her caught her attention, three storeys below, high enough to give her a broader view of the street below but not so high that her view was obscured. She could still make out faces, hair colour, what people were wearing. True, she couldn't have discerned eye colour, but she did have a close enough perspective to get a crude understanding of facial features and expressions and a rudimentary comprehension of what was occurring.

So many days now inside, Sarah had felt them begin to run into one another, but now, looking out her window, watching, observing, spectating, some days soon began to stand out more than others. She began to name the days and sometimes the people, too; she would make up their dialogue because she was too far away to hear what was coming out of their mouths.

"I'm going to tell you about the days that stood out more than the others," Lily could hear Sarah's voice now in her head. "I want to tell you about the scenes that played out in front of me that moved me the most. The ones that stayed with me until the end." Lily could see Sarah's face; it was soft as she said the words, a weathered hand moving to wipe away a tear.

"First, the 'Day of the Lovers'; the soul mates reunited." A smile beamed on Sarah's face as she introduced the first scene, then her face took a back seat to the vibrant scene which Lily could now see herself.

It had been a beautiful, bright day, as though Mother Nature herself had come out to make things perfect. Sarah had noticed the man first; he was waiting impatiently out the front of a house down the road, an older house that Sarah had often looked at and watched as its garden had first become unkept and then overgrown. She'd assumed the tenants had left, but now, as she watched this man emerge from the front door and look around expectantly, she realised that the person living inside it had just been sad, too forlorn to bother about grass and garden beds. But Sarah noticed that his hair was groomed and his face clean-shaven and she would have wagered that until this morning that both of these things had more closely resembled the garden he stood in front of. Sarah watched as his eyes went from his watch to the street, scanning for any oncoming cars or pedestrians, back and forth, impatient, anticipating.

And then, there she was! Sarah watched as the man's patience evaporated and it seemed a weight of sadness lifted from him. A woman had emerged from a taxi a few houses down, a large suitcase in tow; she too looked back and forth for a moment and then seemed to get her bearings, looking towards the man. They began to rush towards each other; for a moment, it may as well have been the clichéd movie scene of the lovers running to each other. She released the handle of her suitcase and reached upwards to meet the embrace of the arms that were reaching down for her. They folded into each other, grasping tightly and fitting perfectly into one another. They kissed for a very long time, then broke apart, laughing and happy. Sarah didn't need to *be able to hear them to understand their story. These two souls were meant for one another, and the universe had separated them for a time for some reason; Sarah would spend many idle hours making up and discarding various scenarios for them having been apart until eventually coming to the conclusion that it didn't matter. In the love story, all that mattered to the viewer was the happy ending, and that's what Sarah got – The happy reunion, the embrace, the kiss, the promise to never part again, the heartbreak turned to happiness. Sarah had watched them go into the house with the unkept garden and noticed with a smile a few weeks later that the lawns were lush and manicured and the gardens now weed-free and in full luscious bloom.*

After this day came many inconsequential days: a bird here and there, a cat, a dog, people walking by. Days not really remembered until 'The Horrible Day' Sarah's face clouded as she spoke the words to Lily. "I've always felt bad about this one, even knowing that if I had run outside to the scene, I still wouldn't have been able to get there in time to stop what happened. I think I felt bad because I didn't even consider going out there. Again, Sarah's face faded in Lily's mind, replaced instead by the vivid image of the scene Sarah had experienced.

The small scruffy child playing on his own at the foot of a street light was an omen, Sarah thought later, well he <u>was</u> ominous; the small form clad in faded and fraying grey, so strange, almost sinister, but his face angelic, his features perfect, like a cartoon drawing or a painting. The street was empty, and still, the day grey like the attire of the boy. Sarah couldn't remember a day quite like this before, so still, the blue of the sky was completely blocked out by the cover of white-grey clouds. It transfixed her and she gazed, absorbed by the lonely tiny boy as he toyed with something she couldn't see on the ground. Of *course, she wondered where his parents or whoever was supposed to be watching him were, even wondering if perhaps they were overseeing him from another vantage point, perhaps a window like hers – but, her thoughts continued, if they were not, if she was, in fact, the only person watching him, hers the only eyes on him, did that mean he had become her charge?*

Her eyes were so fixed on the spot the little stranger sat that she never knew how it had been possible that she hadn't seen him rise and wander into the road. Sarah was ripped out of her abstraction by the screech of tyres that ended in a dull thud, soon to be replaced with a shattering shriek that she would never be able to forget. Sarah thought there were words being uttered inside the scream, but they were indiscernible. There was now a car and a woman in the scene; Sarah could no longer see the boy; the woman was cradling him after having pried him out from under the tyres of the car. There was a flurry of commotion, a driver emerging from the car and frantically gesturing at the woman, speaking to her; the woman looked up to the man, nodding and brushing hair from the angel boy's face. It seemed some consensus had been reached among them and they left together hurriedly in the car. Sarah was never to know why the tiny child with a perfect face had been playing unattended for hours on her street, where his guardian had been or where that screeching car had appeared from. She was also never to acquire a solid confirmation of whether the boy had been okay or if the impact of that car had indeed made that little boy a true angel. Sarah knew she didn't need confirmation; she had seen the way his form had sagged in the woman's arms. She also had seen, though never to admit it even to herself, not even now relaying the story to Lily; Lily saw it anyway; Sarah had seen a grey-white wisp, the same shape as the tiny boy rising from the sagging bundle cradled in the woman's arms, it turned to Sarah for an instant and then continued to rise up until it became indistinguishable from the grey-white of the sky.

After this, Sarah thought it may have been time to stop watching. She pulled down the blind and drew shut the heavy curtains. This was the beginning of a new way of passing her days – listening.

Living in a unit block, the adjoining walls were often the scourge of the tenants, being a source of inefficient noise blocking or a lack of privacy. For Sarah, they became a new connection to worlds outside of her mind and of her safe haven, like the window, allowing her to experience life outside of her apartment without having to let in the fear.

She discovered her new pastime the morning she was woken by a guttural moaning and screaming. She followed the sound, confused, until she reached the blue wall in her lounge room, a wall that until now she had not realised was shared with her next-door neighbour. There was no need for Sarah to press her ear against its flat surface; just being near it was enough; the scream permeating through was primal, raucous; Sarah wasn't sure if someone was being murdered, fucked, or killing someone. Then she heard a second sound, a softer, soothing sound, a voice. Sarah leaned in closer to the wall and tried to make it out, 'Push!' it was someone saying 'push' and hearing this, it dawned on Sarah, just moments before the confirming new sound: the piercing 'waa, waa' that she was hearing someone give birth. And so, this day became 'The Birthday'."

This discovery of another portal into the world outside her home led her to test out the walls on the opposite side of her apartment, the far wall inside her bedroom. Pressing her ear against it and holding her breath for a moment, Sarah could make out the faint sounds of a television program and a couple talking. For the next, however many, countless years, Sarah went back and forth between these two walls, listening and following the lives of the people she could hear. To her, they became not 'wall one' and 'wall two' but 'The family wall 'and 'The Couple wall'. She followed their life journeys, getting to know them, conjuring faces for them and even imagining their lives outside of their homes. Like on the day baby Milly, no longer a baby, went to preschool for the first time, Sarah could clearly see in her mind the chubby brown cheeks and the tight curly spirals of her black hair framing them, her dress and shoes yellow, her favourite colour, her little backpack pink with yellow daisies, her smile excited for her first day as a big girl. Some more years later, Sarah had a tear in her eye, along with Milly's mother, on the day that she left home to attend university in another state. Between these days, Sarah had shared in the happy sounds of many birthdays and family dinners, Christmas mornings and celebrations of all types of milestones. She had also been in attendance for the inevitable family arguments that came with a child's ageing, but none of them so momentous as to stay in Sarah's memory until the end or even for them to get a catalogue card in her mind.

 Sarah became just as familiar with the couple at 'the couple wall' as she did with Milly and her family; she grew to love Lillian and John, their predictable daily routines a comfort to her, their occasional arguments always ending in apologies and making up, the closure satisfying and soothing to Sarah. She listened to the music they listened to, though they never played it obnoxiously loud, just loud enough for Sarah, who was always listening; their reoccurring motif, David Bowie's 'Absolute Beginners' played more often than not and not just occasions like birthdays, anniversaries, or celebrations of whatever, but also just randomly, just because – sometimes both of them singing along, this often turning into laughter and recounted memories, memories that would sometimes lead Sarah to stop listening and move away from the wall, these memories too private for her to feel comfortable listening to. But She did listen through their years of leaving for work and returning home, though never quite able to piece together what it was they actually did; Sarah, in the absence of ever actually knowing, imagined them as teachers, Lillian of primary and John of High school. She celebrated with them when they had a small party to celebrate their retirement and listened to them discussing their many plans for retirement, all of which were things they were to do together. Sarah heard their comings and goings for a few years, leaving and returning from trips with happy laughter and recountings of their favourite parts; she even listened with happiness for them to the days they did nothing but stay home and relax. Sarah started to become concerned when these quiet days at home days seemed to outweigh the more adventurous days; then she overheard a terrible conversation: John had cancer and Lillian had the onset of dementia.

"I'm not going to spend my last days sick and hooked up to machines; I'm not going to die in hospital!" It was the first time Sarah had heard John raise his voice in a while. "I know you want to look after me, but soon you won't be able to; you won't even be able to look after yourself!" There was a brief silence when John was finished speaking.

"I'm dying, you're dying, it's going to be long and drawn out for both of us, we're going to end up separated, our last days will be spent apart, one of us will die, and then the other will be left alone, to die soon after anyway." Lillian, too, was getting *angry.*

"Well, we have options." Sarah imagined John actually smiled when he said that, and when Lillian realised that he'd caught on to what she was thinking but didn't know how to suggest, she smiled too.

"Yes, we do have options; let's take control back. I've never wanted to live without you anyway. I never planned on either of us ending up in a home, and I am not going to let either one of us die in a hospital!" They were both serious now; John looked at Lillian and said.

"I've loved my life with you, Lillian; there's no life without you in it. I wasn't going to suggest it because I didn't want you to do it just because of me. Don't let me sway your decision; you're strong; I'm sure you could go on without me; you could still have life in a care facility," John put forward.

"No," She interrupted, "no, that's not a life. I'm strong because of you; I don't want to find out if I can be strong without you; I don't even care if I am! Even if I wasn't losing my mind, I don't want a life without you in it! We're both dying anyway; we may as well go out on our own terms," Lillian said firmly and with a little shouting.

"But isn't pain and loss a part of life and love? Didn't you always tell me that?" John said softly, warmly.

"No, well yes, but that's for while you're still living, and for self-help books, not for now, when we've almost finished our lives! This is our reality; we don't need to end it with pain and suffering and loneliness; we can end it like Romeo and Juliet if we want to... but with much less teen angst, not a silly misunderstanding, much more well-thought-out," Lillian said, she was firm, and both of them knew a decision had been made.

Sarah heard movement and she knew they were moving

towards each other to embrace. She moved away from the wall to give them some privacy, but she listened anxiously over the next few weeks. A month later, Sarah heard some of a conversation—

"I love the life that we've had together, John; I love every single moment of everything we went through, even the bad things, even the hard things, because all of it was us and I still had you..." It was Lillian's voice.

"I know, I feel the same way; we did so much, we learnt so much, and we cared for each other so deeply, and that isn't ending. I would not have made it this far without you, my darling; I love you so much. I wish we could have had a better ending, a happier ending," John said to her.

"No, John, it is a happy ending. We're here together, and we're ending together; I love you so much; I have never loved anyone or anything more." Lillian was crying, so was John, but it wasn't sadness; it was actually more happiness and relief, relief that they would never live one day, one minute without each other.

"And our love did soar over mountains and hard times; it was just like a film," John told her as he picked up the vials of morphine he'd been saving for a week and the two of them moved to their bed. When Sarah heard 'Absolute beginners' begin to play, she knew the couple were on their final journey together.

The song played through three more times, its lyrics so perfect for them.

And when it ended for the last time, Sarah new that Lillian and John had left together."

Lily turned to Hannah, a tear in her eye but a small smile on her face.

"I'm sorry I can't stay to tell you the end of Sarah's story, but the rest of it is in here." Lily handed Hannah a brown leather-bound notebook. Embossed on its cover were the words Sarah's Death, her final story – her years inside and the things she saw and heard.

"It's up to you now; you have to put together all the stories I've told you; there are copies of them in this." Lily held out a second notebook, this one black and the words on its cover said: Lily's stories, told to her by friendly spirits, to be retold so they live forever.

"I'm sorry I can't stay to help you finish, but I know you can do it; compile the stories and publish them on my blog, then contact Preston Publishing's self-publishing department – there's enough money in here to publish a thousand copies, please make sure they get to people, whether they're sold or given away, that doesn't matter, it's just the stories that matter. That's what it's always been about. You can use whatever you want for your research project, with my permission; there's a written signed consent form here, too." Lily handed a fat envelope to Hannah. "If people ask, and they will, please make sure they know that I wasn't- I mean, I'm not just a psychic, I'm a storyteller, a vessel for their stories. It doesn't matter why these stories; they just are. Everyone's story matters and these were my favourites of the ones that I was lucky enough to tell."

"I really need to go now, Hannah; thank you for your help." Lily rubbed Hannah's arm as she turned to leave, but Hannah didn't feel her touch. Instead, she felt a cold spot where Lily's hand had been; she looked up at Lily, expecting her to head towards the door. Instead, Hannah's eyes followed Lily as she moved towards the Couple Wall; as she reached it, a man's hand was reaching out to her, beckoning; she went to it and took it in her own, then she turned to Hannah one last time, her smiling face became lined and worn, her hair turned to grey, then Hannah could see the wall through her, a Lily shaped outline against the plaster, Lily nodded and smiled at Hannah, giving a final wave as she moved through the wall, Hannah suddenly realised that lily was short for Lillian and she'd gone to be with her John. And then she could hear music, their song; it played for a minute and then got loud enough so that she could hear the words, and she could hear them singing along.

She laid her hand on the wall for a moment. "Thank you, Lily," she whispered. "I'll tell everyone your story." She promised through tears that flowed for both happiness and sorrow, happiness for Lily's release and her return to rest with her true love, John, and sorrow at having to say goodbye to her wonderful friend.

Hannah left with the reluctance of their final goodbye still fresh but also with an eagerness to read the rest of Sarah's story and fulfil Lily's last wish.

Hours later, Hannah sat cross-legged on the floor of her on-campus housing room and opened the first book Lily had handed her. She had been trying to stop thinking about how it had all happened, how any of the last three weeks had been possible, but now she was telling herself to stop questioning it; it had happened and that was all that mattered, like the stories, they just were, and so she eagerly read the ending of Sarah's.

Lily had written:

Sarah's Death

I can't say how Sarah died because she doesn't know herself; she just went to bed one night and didn't wake up. She's not even sure how old she was because she lost track of the days and hours;

she'd stopped checking the date and the time because it had become an intrusion to her carefully crafted insulation; when you never leave the house, time doesn't really matter. After the death of the couple, Sarah had retreated from listening to the outside world, just as she had retreated from looking at it the day the strange little boy had died. She went back to her books for a while and then for a time, she lived inside the worlds of the many films she owned on DVD. Sarah told me not to be sad for her; she says she stopped being sad a long time ago; she was happy just being and now that she's been able to tell her story, so many days now inside, all those days, some more memorable than others, her story that includes all those other stories, witnessed and heard, read and watched from her safe haven, that story, her story can go out into the world, she is content with that and can rest easy now.

*

Hannah shut the notebook and rose to answer a knock at the door. There was no one there, but a box had been left on the floor; taking it inside, for a moment, she thought she could sense Lily nearby. When she unpacked it, she knew why. The box contained a large and well-worn tome that she immediately recognised as the book passed down from generation to generation of storekeepers and tellers in Lily's family; there were also two large pouches, one containing an assortment of gemstones and the other holding the pieces of jewellery she had seen Lily wearing every day. Tied to the drawstring of one of the pouches was a gift tag; it read: Something tangible for you to hold onto. Underneath all of these, at the bottom of the box, was an envelope with her name on it; she opened it and read;

Dear Hannah,

Thank you for helping me. I hope this answers your question as to whether you have any kind of psychic abilities. It seems you are a powerful medium.

Maybe I'll see you again sometime ;)

Love Lily.

Epilogue

Hannah knew she wouldn't see Lily again; that last glance she'd given her over her shoulder before taking John's hand was the last time she'd ever see her. Lily was gone now, her story told, her energy spent; now she was free and would lay resting peacefully with John forever.

But her legacy would live on; what Lily had shared with Hannah allowed her to write an award-winning dissertation and achieve her PhD in the field of parapsychology. When Hannah went to Preston Publishing as instructed by Lily, there was no self-publishing to be paid for; instead, there was a book deal with an advance and all royalties signed to her as the beneficiary. That wasn't all Lily left Hannah either; the apartment that Lily had lived and died in with John, the one sharing the adjoining wall with Sarah's apartment, had been left to her also, and in it was Lily's entire archive of thousands and thousands of stories.

So, although Hannah never saw Lily again, she definitely thought of her from time to time, and she could feel her often.

The End.